PRAISE FOR *THE APOCALYPSE OF ELENA MENDOZA*

★ "Surreal, brainy, and totally captivating."–*Booklist*, starred review

★ "Provocative and moving . . . A thoughtful story about choice and destiny." –*Publishers Weekly*, starred review

★ "Hutchinson artfully blends the realistic and the surreal. . . . An entirely original take on apocalyptic fiction."
–*School Library Journal*, starred review

PRAISE FOR *AT THE EDGE OF THE UNIVERSE*

★ "An earthy, existential coming-of-age gem."
–*Kirkus Reviews*, starred review

★ "While Shaun David Hutchinson (*We Are the Ants*) is a master of fusing the bizarre with the mundane, and the plot is delightfully constructed, it is Ozzie's pained, sardonic voice that steals the spotlight."–*Shelf Awareness*, starred review

"Wrenching and thought-provoking,Hutchinson has penned another winner."–*Booklist*

PRAISE FOR *WE ARE THE ANTS*

★ "Hutchinson has crafted an unflinching portrait of the pain and confusion of young love and loss, thoughtfully exploring topics like dementia, abuse, sexuality, and suicide as they entwine with the messy work of growing up."–*Publishers Weekly*, starred review

★ "Bitterly funny, with a ray of hope amid bleakness."
–*Kirkus Reviews*, starred review

"A beautiful, masterfully told story by someone who is at the top of his craft."–*Lambda Literary*

★ "Shaun David Hutchinson's bracingly smart and unusual YA novel blends existential despair with exploding planets."
–*Shelf Awareness*, starred review

The PAST and OTHER THINGS THAT SHOULD STAY BURIED

SHAUN DAVID HUTCHINSON

SIMON PULSE | NEW YORK LONDON TORONTO SYDNEY NEW DELHI

SIMON PULSE

An imprint of Simon & Schuster Children's Publishing Division
1230 Avenue of the Americas, New York, New York 10020
First Simon Pulse hardcover edition February 2019
Text copyright © 2019 by Shaun David Hutchinson
Jacket art copyright © 2019 by Jon Contino
Interior emoji illustrations copyright © 2019 by Iefym Turkin/iStock
All rights reserved, including the right of reproduction in whole or in part in any form.
SIMON PULSE and colophon are registered trademarks of Simon & Schuster, Inc.
For information about special discounts for bulk purchases, please contact Simon & Schuster
Special Sales at 1-866-506-1949 or business@simonandschuster.com.
The Simon & Schuster Speakers Bureau can bring authors to your live event.
For more information or to book an event contact the Simon & Schuster Speakers Bureau
at 1-866-248-3049 or visit our website at www.simonspeakers.com.
Jacket designed by Sarah Creech
Interior designed by Mike Rosamilia
The text of this book was set in Chaparral Pro.
Manufactured in the United States of America
2 4 6 8 10 9 7 5 3 1
Library of Congress Cataloging-in-Publication Data
Names: Hutchinson, Shaun David, author.
Title: The past and other things that should stay buried / by Shaun David Hutchinson.
Description: First Simon Pulse hardcover edition. | New York : Simon Pulse, 2019. | Summary:
Dino and July, seventeen, are granted time to resolve what was left unfinished between them after
July's sudden death, one year after their friendship ended over Dino's new relationship.
Identifiers: LCCN 2018009640 (print) | LCCN 2018017187 (eBook) |
ISBN 9781481498579 (hardcover : alk. paper) | ISBN 9781481498593 (eBook)
Subjects: | CYAC: Dead—Fiction. | Future life—Fiction. | Best friends—Fiction. |
Friendship—Fiction. | Undertakers and undertaking—Fiction. |
Funeral homes—Fiction. | Gays—Fiction.
Classification: LCC PZ7.H96183 (eBook) | LCC PZ7.H96183 Pas 2019 (print) |
DDC [Fic]—dc23
LC record available at https://lccn.loc.gov/2018009640

FOR RACHEL, WHO KNOWS WHERE
ALL THE BODIES ARE BURIED

DINO

I DON'T WANT TO BE HERE. SPENDING THE AFTERNOON collecting trash on the beach isn't how I wanted to spend one, or any, of my summer days. I could be sleeping or working at a job that pays me or reading or smack-talking some random kid while I kick his butt at *Paradox Legion* online. Instead, I'm here. At the beach. Picking up beer cans and candy wrappers and ignoring the occasional used condom because there's no way I'm touching that. Not even wearing gloves.

Dear People:
If you have sex on the beach, throw away your own goddamn condoms.
Sincerely,
Sick of Picking Up Your Rubbers

"Hey, Dino!"

I look up.

"Smile!" Rafi Merza snaps a picture of me with his phone, and I'm not fast enough to give him the finger.

"Jerk."

Rafi shrugs and wraps his arm around my waist and slaps a kiss on my cheek. His carefully cultivated stubble scrubs my skin. Everything about Rafi is intentional and precise. His thick black hair swooped up and back to give it the illusion of messiness, his pink tank top to highlight his thick arms, the board shorts he thinks make his ass look good. He's right; they do. It's showing off. If I looked like Rafi, I'd want to flaunt it too. Thankfully there's an underlying insecurity to his vanity that keeps it from slipping across the border into narcissism.

"You okay?"

"I'm fine," I say. "People need to worry about themselves." I point down the beach at Dafne and Jamal, who're poking at a gelatinous mass in the sand. "I hope they know jellyfish can still sting even when they're dead."

"They'll find out one way or another." Rafi has a hint of an accent that sounds vaguely British with weird New England undertones, which makes sense since his dad's from Boston and his mom's from Pakistan by way of London.

"And I'll keep my phone out just in case," I say.

"To call the paramedics?"

"To record them getting stung."

Rafi pulls away from me. "Sure, because there's nothing funnier than someone else's pain."

"They're playing with a jellyfish, not a live grenade."

He nudges me and I catch my reflection in his sunglasses. My enormous bobble head and long nose and I don't even know what the hell's going on with my hair. "No one dragged you out here—"

"You showed up at my house at dawn with coffee and doughnuts," I say. "You know I can't resist doughnuts."

Rafi tries to take my hand, but I shake free. "I get that today's difficult for you, Dino—"

"Please don't."

"I'm here for you." Rafi raises his shades, giving me the amber-eyed puppy dog stare that snared me from across an Apple store a year ago. "If you want, we can take off and go somewhere to talk."

Looking across the beach and then into Rafi's eyes makes the offer so tempting that I go so far as to open my mouth to say yes. But then I don't. "July Cooper is dead. Talking won't change it." I kick the wet sand, sending a clod flying toward the water. "Besides, we weren't even friends."

Rafi leans his forehead against mine. He's a little shorter than me, so I have to bend down a bit. "I'm your friend, right?"

"Of course you are."

"And so are they." He doesn't have to motion to them for me to know he's talking about everyone else who's out here with us on a summer day cleaning the beach. The kids from the community center: Kandis and Jamal and Charlie and Dafne and Leon. "They're your family."

"I've got a family," I say.

Rafi kisses me softly. His lips barely graze mine, and still I flinch from the public display, but if Rafi notices, he doesn't mention it. "That's the family you were born into. We're the family you chose."

There's a moment where I feel like Rafi expects me to say something or that there's something *he's* trying to say. It charges the air between us like we're the two poles of a Jacob's ladder. But either I imagined it or the moment passes, because Rafi steps away and starts walking down the shore, linking his first finger through mine and pulling me along with him.

The sun beats on us as we keep working to clean the beach. It's an impossible task but still worthwhile. My arms and legs are pink, and I have to stop to apply more sunscreen. I try to convince Rafi to put some on too, but he claims it defeats the purpose of summer. I'm kind of jealous of the way Rafi's skin turns a rich brown in the sun rather than a crispy red like mine.

"Don't forget about the party tonight," Rafi says as he rubs sunscreen into my back.

"What party?"

"It's not actually a party. The gang, pizza, pool, movies. Nothing too exciting."

My whole body tenses, and Rafi must feel it because he stops rubbing. "You don't have to come. I thought it'd be better than sitting home alone."

"The funeral's tomorrow, so I should probably—"

"I get it—"

"It's not that I don't want to see you—"

"Of course, of course."

This time there's no electricity in the silence. No expectation. Instead, it's a void. A chasm growing wider with each passing second. I know I should throw Rafi a line before the distance between us expands too far, but I don't know what to say.

"My offer stands," Rafi says.

I sigh heavily without meaning to. "If I change my mind about the party—"

"Not the party. The funeral. If you want me to go with you, I will."

"You don't have to."

"Have you ever seen me in my black suit?" he asks. "I look like James Bond. But, you know, browner."

I can't help laughing because it's impossible to tell whether Rafi's bragging or begging for compliments. "While the thought of you doing your best sexy secret agent impersonation is tempting, I think I need to go to the funeral alone."

Rafi squeezes my shoulders and says, "Yeah, okay," before finishing with the sunscreen. Funerals are awful, especially if you don't know the person who's died, but I can't help feeling like Rafi's disappointed.

"Come on," I say. "I probably need to get home soon." I pull Rafi the way he pulled me earlier, but instead of following, he digs his feet into the sand. His lips are turned down, and he's looking at the ground instead of at my face.

I covertly glance around to make sure no one's watching, and then I brush his cheek with my thumb and kiss him. "Fine. I'll consider coming tonight."

Rafi's face brightens immediately. He goes from pouty lips to dimples and smiles in under a second. "Really?"

"Maybe," I say.

"Maybe closer to yes or maybe closer to no?"

This time when I kiss him, I don't care if we've got an audience. "Maybe if you agree to go with me to Kennedy Space Center before the end of the summer, I'll think real hard about making an appearance."

Rafi turns up his nose. "But I went there in middle school, and it's *so* boring."

"Compromise is the price you pay for being my boyfriend."

"Fine." Rafi rolls his eyes dramatically. "But this relationship is getting pretty expensive."

"You're rich. You can afford it." I grab his hand. "Now, let's get out of here before I change my mind."

DINO

I'M SITTING AT THE KITCHEN TABLE TRYING TO EAT DINNER when my mom stomps into the room and twirls. "Think this is okay for dinner with the Kangs tonight?" She's wearing a black dress with a fitted corset top that accentuates her curvy hips, black fishnet stockings, and combat boots, and she even straightened her platinum blond hair for the occasion. Both of her arms are covered in tattoos depicting scenes from her favorite comic books.

"Are you taking them to a club in the 1990s?"

"Smartass." My mom's basically goth Peter Pan, but I admire her devotion to the Church of Monochromism.

"Kidding. You look nice."

Mom smiles and kisses the top of my head. "What're you doing?"

I hold up my spoon. "Eating dinner."

"Cereal is not dinner."

"Then I'm eating a meal that's not dinner but will take the place of dinner tonight."

"You were supposed to get your dad's sense of humor and *my* sense of fashion, not the reverse."

I glance at my outfit. I'd showered and changed into a T-shirt and jean shorts when I got home from the beach. "Are you criticizing my style?"

Mom pats my cheek. "Kid, the way you dress isn't style in the same way that cereal isn't dinner."

"Ouch," I say. "This coming from the woman who believes that all clothes, shoes, and makeup should come in one and only one color."

"Hey! I have a blue dress up there." Mom taps her chin. "Somewhere." I'm hoping she's going to disappear the way she came, but she pulls out a chair and sits across from me. "How you holding up?"

"I'd be better if people would stop asking me that."

"July was your best friend."

"Was," I say. "But she's been dead to me for a year, so can you drop it?" My left fist starts trembling, and I have to drop my spoon because I didn't realize I was gripping it so tightly. These last few days it feels like everyone's waiting for me to melt down, and I'm starting to think they're not going to leave me alone until I do. But, no. I'm not going to give them the satisfaction of doing the thing they presume is inevitable. "I'm fine."

Mom watches me for a moment and then nods. "After . . . everything's done, I could use your help in the office. We've got

Mr. Alire out there now, and Mrs. Lunievicz is being transported over tomorrow."

"I already have a summer job."

"Bussing tables at a diner isn't a job."

My eyebrows dip as I frown. "I spend a set amount of time at a place performing tasks dictated to me by a supervisor in exchange for an established wage." I pause and look up. "Sounds like the definition of a job to me."

Mom's hands explode with motion as she speaks. "You're wasting your talent!"

"It's my talent to waste."

"When it comes to preparing bodies, I'm good, and Dee's even better, but you could be van Gogh!" There are few things that get my mom's cold, black heart beating. Concrete Blonde popping up on shuffle, a sale on black boots, a new Anne Rice novel, and talking about my potential.

"Van Gogh was considered a failure and a madman who ultimately took his own life. I'd hardly call him an appropriate role model."

"Why can't you be more like your sister?" Mom says.

Speaking of perfect offspring, Delilah waltzes through the kitchen door. She got my mom's hourglass figure and my dad's sunny disposition. She's the optimal genetic mix of our parents. I wish I could hate her for it but . . . Oh, who am I kidding? I totally hate her for it.

"Because then I wouldn't be me," I say to Mom, ignoring Dee for the moment. "And aren't you the one who drilled into us the importance of owning and loving who we are? Well this is me. I eat cereal for dinner, I dress like a slob, and I plan to waste my summer cleaning strangers' dirty tables."

Mom clenches her jaw as she slowly stands. She hugs Delilah and says, "I'm going to check on your father. We'll leave in an hour."

Dee nods. When Mom is gone, she strips off her white coat, tosses it over the back of the chair, and takes Mom's place at the table. "Do I want to know what that was about?"

It takes a few seconds for my body to relax and my muscles to unclench. "I'm wasting my potential, blah, blah, blah; I'm a disappointment, etcetera." I roll my eyes.

"You're not a disappointment." Dee frowns, but it's not a natural expression for her. My sister glided out of the birth canal on a rainbow, armed with an angelic smile that bestows blessings upon anyone fortunate enough to glimpse it. "You wanna talk?"

"I swear to God if one more person asks me if I'm okay or if I need to talk or if I'm upset about July, I'm going to burn this house to the ground."

"Mental note," Dee says. "Hide the lighters."

"I was a Boy Scout; I don't need a lighter." I get up, dump the rest of my dinner down the drain, and rinse my bowl in the sink. I flip on the garbage disposal and use the grinding hum to re-center myself and come up with a way to steer the conversation away from my mental state. "You nervous about Mom and Dad meeting Theo's parents?" I ask when I return to my seat.

Delilah groans and scrubs her face with her hands. "The Kangs are awesome. It's our parents I'm worried about."

"Ten bucks Dad brings up skin slippage before the entrées."

"I'll murder him if he does." Dee's eyes narrow and her lips pucker. She doesn't get angry often, but I'm familiar with the signs. I consider warning Mom to keep the sharp knives away from my sister, but nah. If Dee stabs them, it'll be because they deserve it. "Do you remember what Dad told you the first time you asked him why people have to die?"

I frown, trying to recall it. "No."

She clears her throat and says, "*Death is as normal as digestion. People move through life the way food moves through our bodies. Their natural usefulness is extracted along the way to help enrich the world, and when they have nothing left to give, they're eliminated. Much like our bodies would clog up with excrement if we didn't defecate, the world would do the same if we didn't die.*" Her impression of our father is scarily accurate.

I bust up laughing, which infects Dee, and once she gets started, it turns into a storm of snorting and donkey hee-haws that causes me to completely lose it until we must sound to Mom and Dad upstairs like we're torturing farm animals. I clutch my side as I stand to get a paper towel to dab the tears from my eyes.

"How did either of us turn out so normal?" Delilah asks. Her cheeks are flush with joy where I just look splotchy.

"Who says we did? You're a fusion of their weirdest parts, and I have no idea what I'm doing with my life."

Delilah reaches across the table and rests her hand on mine. "You'll figure it out, Dino. You always do." She smiles. "And if you don't want to work here, don't."

"It's DeLuca and *Son's*," I say.

"Names can be changed."

I sigh. "It's going to be weird not having you in the house once you're married."

"I won't be far," Delilah says. "We're planning to tell the parents at dinner, but Theo and I closed on a house last week that's only twenty minutes from here."

"Great," I say. "Now I'll never get rid of you."

"Probably not."

"So you're really marrying Theo, huh?" The Wedding has ruled our lives for the last six months. Not a day goes by when there isn't something that needs to be decided or tasted or fitted. But Theo's a cool guy, and he loves my sister, which proves that there really is someone for everyone, even overachieving perfectionists who spend their days with the dead.

Delilah leans back in her chair. "That's what the invitations say."

"I thought they said you where marrying Thea?"

"Those were the old invitations."

"Thea's going to be disappointed."

"She'll move on." Dee glances at the time on the microwave. "And I should be doing the same. Can't show up to dinner smelling like corpses."

I fidget with my thumbs. "How do you know you're in love with Theo?"

Delilah freezes for a moment, narrows her eyes. "Is this about Rafi? Are you in love with him?"

I shake my head. "Just curious."

She relaxes, but there's a second where I think she's not going to answer. It was a stupid question anyway. But then she says, "You know how I used to keep that map on my wall with the thumbtacks in each place I wanted to visit?"

"Yeah?"

"When I couldn't sleep, I'd stare at the map and imagine the adventures I'd go on. Backpacking through Bangkok, watching the stars from Iceland, eating noodles in Shanghai. But in those fantasies, I was alone."

"That's because you didn't have any friends."

Delilah slaps my arm. "I had friends!"

"Dad doesn't count."

"Jerk." Dee shakes her head at me. "Anyway. Theo and I had been dating for a couple of years, and I was in bed and couldn't sleep, so I started thinking about that map and the places I wanted to go. Only, this time I wasn't alone on my journeys. Theo was with me. He'd slipped into my life, and now I can't imagine my life without him."

"Gross." I mime puking onto the floor and even make the gagging sounds to go with it.

Delilah stands for real this time. "Love's only gross when you're not in it."

DINO

PEOPLE, LIKE CATS, ARE OBSESSED WITH BOXES. CATS are content to squeeze their own furry asses into boxes clearly too small for them, whereas humans take sadistic pleasure in trying to shove one another into boxes. Slut boxes and Bitch boxes and Nerd boxes and Thug boxes. "He was such a nice" white boys often get to pick their own luxury boxes, unless they don't fit sexuality or gender norms, in which case they're crammed into Fag boxes and tossed out with the Trash boxes.

We claim this type of forced categorization provides us the ability to define our place in the world, and that, paradoxically, it's what's on the inside that truly counts. But once we stuff someone into a box, what's on the inside no longer matters. The boxes that are supposed to help us understand one another ultimately wedge us further apart. Even worse is that we rage against the artificial divisions the boxes create, claim that we're more complex and complicated than how we're defined by others, and then turn around and stuff the next person we meet into one and tape the lid shut.

And then, as if the indignity of life isn't enough, when a person dies, we cram what's left of them into one final box for eternity.

I thought I knew everything there was to know about July Cooper and that she'd known all there was to know about me. We'd spent more than half of our seventeen years on earth together, spreading the contents of who we were across Palm Shores, marveling at the complexities of one another. Then in one moment, I swept her up, crammed her into a box, closed it, and wrote "Ex–Best Friend" on the outside. And she did the same to me.

But boxes are meant to be unpacked. They're not intended to be filled and shut and stuffed into a dark corner to rot. If someone had asked me a month ago how I felt about July Cooper, I would have told them I didn't care, but now that she's gone, I want to unpack her. To unpack us and the myriad crap we stuffed into each other's boxes. I can't, though, and that's my fault. But I can see her one last time.

As soon as Mom and Dad and Dee leave to meet the Kangs for dinner, I walk across the lawn to the office and let myself into the prep room. I never go through the showroom unless I have no other choice.

Most people believe the preparation room is the creepiest part of a mortuary. The process of embalming bodies and readying them for burial sounds ghoulish to them, but that aspect of the business doesn't bother me. What I find grotesque is how people empty their wallets for caskets they're going to spend a couple hours looking at before burying them in the ground. It's not like they're burying fine art that's going to appreciate in value over time and that they can exhume in twenty years. They'd be better off digging a hole, throwing stacks of cash inside, and burying that instead.

The prep room is stainless steel and impeccably clean, which makes sense seeing as Dee was the last person to leave; her nightly cleaning ritual borders on obsessive. Two large sinks dominate one wall, with metal embalming tables at the stations, empty but ready for use; the other wall is covered with cabinets containing chemicals and tools of the trade; a small desk sits in the corner; and a large freezer takes up most of the space on the far side of the room. All of it lit by bright halogen bulbs instead of those flickering fluorescents that make even the living look dead.

See? Nothing creepy about the prep room, and it's cleaner than most restaurant kitchens.

I open the freezer door. There are two bodies inside.

The meatsicle on the first gurney belongs to Mr. Alire. He died of a heart attack at the age of ninety-four, leaving behind his wife, three children, and seven grandchildren. I learned from his obituary that he served in World War II and then in the Korean War in counterintelligence. After leaving the military, he traveled the world as a photographer, went to college, invented some type of light sensor for cameras that made him rich, and eventually retired to Palm Shores to spend his twilight years in "paradise."

Waiting to make her big debut on gurney number two lies July Cooper. Death by surprise aneurism at the age of seventeen. According to the medical examiner's report, July's death would have happened eventually. The artery in her brain that failed had been weak since birth, and it was a miracle she'd lived as long as she did. But life probably doesn't feel like a miracle to the dead, and it sure as hell doesn't feel like one to those of us left behind.

What am I doing?

I pull July's gurney out of the freezer and wheel it to one of the prep stations. Her body is covered with a sheet that I fold down to her shoulders. Dee must've already started preparing the body—putting on makeup and brushing her hair—except she made July's lips too dark and the shade of her skin a little too light. I don't know why I care. Even now, colonies of natural bacteria in her body are spreading, eating her muscles and fat, breaking her down. The only way to arrest that process is to embalm her. To scoop out her guts and paint on her face and stick a candle in her to imitate life. Like a jack-o'-lantern. Thankfully, the Coopers requested a chemical-free burial.

Rationally, I know that the meat defrosting on the table used to be the girl I told my secrets to. The girl who cried in my arms when her parents got divorced, the girl who made my coming out about her, the girl I watched movies with and fought with and made up with. My brain is telling me that this is the girl who used to dip her french fries in mayonnaise and who refused to shave her armpits and legs throughout eighth grade to spite

Mr. Fowler for telling her it was unladylike to do otherwise, and who went with me to the fair every year, even though she hated it, so that I didn't have to ride the rides alone.

But my heart keeps saying this can't be her. That she's on the other side of Palm Shores, in her bedroom watching *Hairspray* for the millionth time, cooking up some new scheme to humiliate me, and that I'll see her at Publix one day or in school for our senior year in August.

My heart won't believe this is July because that means the last words I said to her were "Good luck" and she died thinking I hated her.

I don't know if I hated her before, and I've lost the chance to find out for certain, but I know that I hate her now.

"I hate you for dying, July. I hate that stupid weak artery in your brain and the paramedics for not getting to you quickly enough and the doctors in the ER for not saving you." My voice is barely a whisper, but it's not like it matters. I could shred my throat shouting at her and July wouldn't hear me.

I grab Delilah's makeup kit from the cabinet and dig through it for a foundation that matches July's skin tone better. I think her dad had some Greek in his background that gave her a bronzy complexion. No matter the time of year, she looked like she'd recently returned from a week soaking up the sun on a private island.

I pop my earbuds in and queue up some music on my phone. The first song starts, and it's angsty screeching, which, while appropriate, isn't what I'm in the mood for, so I search through my playlists until I find the one July and I made for our first day of high school. It's nonstop electronic pop and bubblegum boy bands, and it's embarrassingly bad, but I crank the volume and get to work making July presentable.

The trick to putting makeup on a dead body without getting skeeved out is to forget that it's a body. To focus on drawing the lines of the lips just right or on smoothing out the blemishes on the forehead, and to absolutely ignore the stitches at the edge of the hairline where the skull was sawed through for the autopsy or the puckered lines at her shoulders that disappear under the sheet. Most of the time we work from a photograph—and most of the time the photograph is of the person twenty years ago because every family member wants the body to look their best, which, whatever; we do makeup, not time travel—but I know July's face better than any picture. I lose myself in the work. As much as I hate admitting that Mom's right, I *am* good at this. It's not what I see myself doing for the rest of my life, but it's what I'm doing for now.

My pocket buzzes and I jump. I nearly fumble my phone getting it out and am disappointed when it's only a text from Rafi.

Rafi's inability to capitalize or punctuate his sentences in texts drives me mad. When we started dating, he constantly pointed out that I sounded angry when I ended sentences with periods, so now I sprinkle random emojis throughout to help him understand my emotional state.

RAFI: how you doing
RAFI: not like that
RAFI: in general

ME: Fine. 😃

RAFI: think youre coming to the party

RAFI: i bought those little wieners you like

RAFI: please no wiener jokes

ME: I hadn't planned on it. That applies to the party AND the jokes. 😊

RAFI: boooo

RAFI: i miss you

ME: You just saw me.

RAFI: still miss u though

ME: I'll think about it. 😆 😆 🖤

I mute the conversation. He means well, I get that, and I should appreciate that I have a boyfriend who cares so much about me—and I do. But it's complicated. Rafi's part of the reason July and I stopped being friends. I think. Kind of. Like I said: complicated. Either way, being around Rafi while I'm trying to sort out my feelings for July would only confuse me more. It's best to keep him at a distance until after the funeral tomorrow.

I return my attention to July and check out my work. The differences are subtle, but now she looks like the July Cooper I remember. Her round cheeks making her look perpetually like she's on the verge of smiling, her wavy auburn hair, her bright blue eyes—

Eyes? Her eyes are supposed to be closed. They *were* closed. How are they open?

I take a step toward the gurney.

July Cooper sits up and screams.

JULY

SNAP!

It's like that.

I bolt upright and I don't know where I am.

I'm screaming and I don't know why.

So I stop. Except not. No. I'm definitely not screaming.

Oh. It's Dino, looking like a shaved llama in a Star Wars T-shirt, his bug eyes wide, yowling like someone gutted him. But why's he here?

"Dino?"

He'd probably keep backing up until he hit the ocean, but he runs into the wall and points at me and says, "You're dead!"

"Am not." But then I look down and see I'm on a metal table in the DeLuca's chop shop, and I peek under the sheet I'm wearing and there are two cuts that run across the tops of my breasts, meet at my sternum, and keep doing down. I pull the blanket tighter against me and shiver even though I don't feel cold. I don't feel anything.

"What the fuck is going on?" I demand. "You better answer me, or so help me God, I will beat your flat ass concave."

"You're dead," he says again. "You died. How is this possible?"

"Fine," I say. "Don't answer. I'm outta here." I slide off the table and march toward the door.

"What're you doing? Get back on the table."

"Make me."

"You're dead, July!" This time when he says it, the words stop me short. My hand hovers over the doorknob. "Four days ago you had an aneurism. You were at home eating dinner with your mom and sister, and then you died."

I don't turn. Not yet. "Why am I here?"

"Because your funeral's tomorrow. There was an autopsy and then they brought you here, and this can't be happening." There's panic in his voice, like the time we got caught sneaking home from a party when his parents thought we were sleeping in his room. "We're supposed to be burying you tomorrow."

I round on him. "You are not burying me alive."

"You're not alive!"

"Then what the hell am I?"

"I don't know!" Dino moves to the nearest chair and falls into it. Some of the fluster blows out of him. "I don't know."

"I can't be dead," I say. "We were eating supper, and I was telling Momma how Benji kept screwing up his lines during rehearsals and Mr. Moore was threatening to replace him and then . . ."

"And then what, July?"

"Then . . ." I dig through my memories like they're tangible things. I was complaining to Momma about how Benji was too busy flirting with his understudy to learn the songs and then . . . "And then nothing. I woke up here." I slide to the floor and cry, only no tears come out so I kind of dry-eye shake.

When I'm done crying, I catch Dino staring. He's all trembling like he's scared I'm gonna pounce and make a meal of him. "What?"

"How can you even ask that? You're dead—"

"I'm not dead."

Dino ignores me, as usual. "Do you have a heartbeat? Are you cold?"

I press my hand to my chest, but before I can answer, Dino says, "That's not even where your heart is."

"I might not have gotten an A in biology like some over-achievers in the room—"

"Neither did I, thanks to you."

"—but I know where my heart's supposed to be." I throw him a dirty look and let my hand drop. "What does it matter anyway? Beating, not beating, it doesn't change that I'm sitting here having this ridiculous conversation with you. Therefore, either I'm not dead or this is hell and you're my punishment."

"This shouldn't be happening." He says it more to himself than to me.

"Look at it like a miracle," I say. "I saved your folks from making the horrible mistake of burying me alive."

"You're not alive!"

Arguing is getting us nowhere, so I drop it for now. "Why were you down here, anyway? And how come I'm naked? You sneak out here to fool around with the bodies? Is that your thing?"

Dino sputters and twitches. "No! That's not my thing! That's not *anyone's* thing." Seeing him flustered makes me smile a little. "I was fixing your makeup for the funeral tomorrow. And you're naked because that's how you were delivered to us." He points at a garment bag hanging in the corner. "Your mom dropped that off for you to be buried in."

"But you don't even like me, so why do you care how I look?" I stab a finger at him. "Got you there, didn't I?"

"You died, July!" he shouts. "Maybe I wanted to see you one last time."

"Uh-oh. Better call the dramahawk 'cause the waaambulance'll take too long to get here." I roll my eyes. "Why don't you cry to your boyfriend so I don't have to hear it?"

"Five minutes. You made it five minutes before bringing up Rafi."

"I'm not the one who ditched his best friend when he got a boyfriend. I could see you bailing on me for Malik Sommers. He's got that smile and that ass and damn! But you left me for some boy I never even met." I let disappointment creep into every corner of my face, giving Dino the full weight of it.

"I invited you to do stuff with us."

"Do I look like your third wheel?"

"You are so frustrating!" Dino bunches up his fists and glares at me like he's got a million more words where that came from, but he keeps them to himself. As usual.

After a minute of silence, I say, "Did someone force you to wear those shorts? They're too tight and no one needs to see that much of your fuzzy legs."

Instead of getting feisty, Dino starts laughing. The loud, rumbling sound of it fills the mortuary. "God, I hate you, July. And I've missed you."

"Feeling is and isn't mutual," I say. "In that order."

"We have to figure out what's going on."

"I'm alive," I say. "What more do you need to know?"

"You're *not* alive!"

"Then what? You think I'm a zombie?"

"No. Maybe. Do you feel a feral desire to eat my brains?"

"Not wanting to eat Spam doesn't mean I'm not hungry."

"Are you comparing my brain to Spam?"

"Don't get uptight about it," I say. "I'm not the one who nearly buried his best friend alive."

"You're not my best friend. Not anymore. And you're not alive."

I sneer at him. "You know what I meant."

Dino's voice is quieter and his eyes have stopped darting toward the exits, but he's still keeping his distance. "You should be grateful your parents decided not to have you embalmed."

"Why?"

"Imagine waking up with spiked caps in your eyes or trying to scream with your mouth sewn shut. And that's the least horrifying orifice they sew closed."

A shiver runs through me even though I don't feel cold. Or hot. It's like the time I had a cavity filled and the doctor used laughing gas on me instead of novocaine. I felt the drilling, but it was like it was happening to someone else. Whatever, I don't want to think about it. "How messed up was everyone when I died? And if they weren't rending their shirts and sobbing into their pillows, lie to me."

"Your parents were a wreck." He bobs his shoulders, stalling for time. "It's summer. I haven't seen anyone else from school."

"Too busy with your boyfriend and your little friends from the shelter?"

"It's a community center," he says. "And can we not talk about Rafi?"

"I'm sensing trouble. Spill it, Dino."

"There's no trouble."

But I keep at him; I can't help myself. "You find out you're both bottoms? That seems like the sort of question you should've asked before blowing off your best friend for him."

Dino pushes himself to his feet and stands over me like a summer storm, swift and furious. "That's not funny, *and* it's none of your business, so shut up about it, okay? Can you do that, or do I need to put you back in the freezer?"

My whole body tenses for a fight, but I keep still because— let's face it—Dino would lose to a bulky sweater, but also because I remember that Dino was always the boy who got angry when he meant to get scared.

A few moments pass with neither of us talking, so I say, "As comfortable as this sheet is, I'd love some real clothes."

Dino watches me suspiciously like he thinks I'm luring him into a trap. Like the moment he stands and turns around I'm going to lunge at him and bite off his nose for a tasty treat. When I don't, he grabs the garment bag from the rack and unzips it, revealing a high-necked blue dress with an Amish collar.

"Over my dead body," I say.

"On your dead body, specifically."

I shake my head so hard I'm worried it's going to fly off my neck. "My folks expected me to wear a blue sack to heaven?"

Dino snorts. "It's hilarious that you expected you were going to heaven. Anyway, it's not that bad, July."

"Anyone ever ask you for fashion advice?" I motion at the tragic outfit Dino put together himself and wore thinking he looked good. "No? Then shut up."

"How can you be worried about clothes when you literally rose from the dead?" Dino asks. I answer in the form of a middle finger; strike that, two middle fingers. "If you feel that strongly about it . . ."

"What?" I use the wall to help me stand.

First he looks constipated, then his jaw falls slack like he's lost whatever conflict was raging in his brain. "You could probably borrow clothes from Dee. For however long . . . this lasts." Then he adds, "You're on your own for eternity."

DINO

I STAND IN THE DOORWAY OF DEE'S BEDROOM WHILE July paws through the clothes in the closet.

"Seriously," July says. "I forgot what a neat freak your sister is."

July isn't wrong. Dee organizes her hanging clothes by type and color, and her bed has sharp hospital corners. "It's going to be a massive shock when she and Theo move in together."

"That's an understatement." July throws an "are you kidding me" look my way. Then she pulls a zip-up University of Florida hoodie out and hangs it on the side of the dresser.

"She stays at his place on the weekends, but they only recently bought a house, so it'll be their first time sharing a place full time."

July lets out a low whistle. "She's braver than me."

"How do you figure?"

"Spending every hour with one person for the rest of my life?

No way. Now, if I could marry someone but maybe still have my own place? I could be down with that."

It's surreal listening to July talk about her life like she's got one to look forward to. I have no idea what's going on—why she's not dead, how any of this is possible, and how long it's going to last—but July's rolling with it like everything's perfectly normal while I'm attempting to do my best impression of someone who's not freaking out that his ex–best friend rose from the dead.

July finally pulls a pair of jeans out of the closet. She has more of a butt than my sister and is a little taller, but my mom's clothes would fit even worse, so these will have to suffice.

I turn around to give July privacy to dress.

"So," July says hesitantly. "You saw my folks?"

"Yeah."

"Joëlle?"

"Yeah."

"How're they holding up?"

"Your mom brought *us* a casserole," I say. "Spinach and ham."

July laughs. "Christ, Momma's got a recipe for everything."

"But she seemed to be keeping it together. Your mom's pretty much—"

"Unbreakable?" I snort. "She got that from Granddaddy. Never let your feelings show in public."

My mom and dad asked me to be there when the Coopers came in so they'd see a friendly face. Mrs. Cooper smiled her way through the details, like she could wear Death down with politeness. "Your dad doesn't seem to have that problem. He was a wreck."

"Damn!" July says. "Is Dee's ass as flat as yours? I can barely get these things on."

"Do you need help?"

"No!"

"I could get some butter. Grease you up first."

"Sure," July says. "And when I'm done you can use it to see how much farther you can stick your head up your own ass." She doesn't speak for a few moments, and all I hear is some huffing and grunting, which I do my best to ignore. Thankfully, Mrs. Cooper brought July's own bra and underwear so that she doesn't have to borrow those from Dee too.

"Daddy can handle a crisis unless it involves his girls. Remember when I had my tonsils out? He had to leave the room when the nurse put in my IV. He can't bear to see us in pain. But it was probably the first time they've been in the same room in a year without fighting."

"It's not like anyone blames him for grieving. He lost a daughter. That would mess any parent up."

July clears her throat. "I'm done."

Not being wrapped in a sheet helps July look less dead. If I squint just right, I can maybe fool my brain into believing she's alive.

"Think Dee'd mind if I borrowed some of her makeup?"

"Yes," I say, resisting the urge to tell her I already did her makeup and that she doesn't need more. It's likely unwise to anger her in case she does get hungry for brains. "But I won't tell if you won't."

July stands in front of the mirror over Delilah's dresser and rubs moisturizer into her arms and hands and face, and then sets to work applying foundation and blush and lipstick and eyeliner and mascara.

"How about Jo?" she asks.

"Do you really want to know?"

July glances at me through the mirror and purses her lips. "Of course. Why would you ask me a dumbass question like that?"

"Because what if this doesn't last?" I ask. "Do you want to hear how badly your little sister is handling you being dead?"

"But I'm not dead anymore."

"You're not alive either," I say. "You can't go talk to her."

"Why not?"

I don't understand what's going on, so I don't know how to make July understand it either, but I have to try. "Pretend you go home and see Jo and tell her life's peachy because you've risen from the dead. And then tomorrow or the next day or the day after that, you die again. How fair is it to give her or your parents hope and then yank it away?"

July's working up an argument; I can tell by the way her jaw's twitching. But all she says is, "She's my sister. I'm worried about her."

Joëlle's thirteen and soon to be a freshman at Palm Shores High, but where July's larger than life, Jo barely registers sometimes.

"I know," I say. "But she survived living with you; eventually she'll figure out how to live without you."

"Hey!" July lobs one of Dee's lipsticks at me, and I duck to avoid it smacking me in the face.

I retrieve the lipstick and return it to the top of Dee's dresser, trying to remember the exact position it was in.

"It's weird talking to you, Dino."

"You too."

July finishes applying eyeliner, sets the pencil down, and faces me. My job was better, but if she wants to look like a circus clown, who am I to argue?

"What now?" she says.

"I don't know. Two hours ago you were in a freezer. In less than twenty-four hours you're supposed be in the ground, and I have no clue what happens if you're not. Aren't walking and talking enough?"

"We should go somewhere," July says like she didn't hear a word I said.

"You. Are. A. Corpse. We have no idea why this is happening or what you even are." I try to take a breath, but the low-level panic that's been buzzing inside of me starts to bust out. "Your heart's not beating, but your eyes are clear and blue when they should be cloudy and flat. Your blood should be pooled in your back or feet, but it's not. You're not breathing, so how are you talking?"

July does that infuriating thing where she gives me duck lips and an "I don't give a crap" frown. "Who cares?"

"I do!"

"Well, I don't, and since I'm the one not-dead, my vote counts double."

"People will freak out if they recognize you."

"Then we'll have to be careful." July pinches my lips shut before I can argue. Her fingers are mushy and rubbery. Not cold but not warm, either.

"This is ridiculous," I mumble. I could try to restrain her, keep her in the prep room, but she's stronger than me. Besides, dead, not-dead, she's still got the right to decide what happens to her, even if she chooses the most illogical course of action. Letting her have her way is the easiest option. It's always been that way between me and July. She wears me down until she gets what she wants. Even in death, nothing's changed.

"Fine," I say. "We'll go for a drive, but we have to be home before my parents."

July pats my cheek. "This'll be fun. I promise."

"You also promised we'd be best friends forever. Look how that turned out."

DINO

I HAVE NO IDEA WHERE I'M DRIVING. PALM SHORES IS not the kind of town people who thrive on excitement choose to live in. The biggest event last year was Starbucks opening a second store. People in Palm Shores may be boring, but they love their lattes. The main road that runs east-west is lined with grocery stores and Chipotles and gas stations. We've got a nice luxury movie theater and a used bookstore. Finding a way to stave off boredom usually means leaving Palm Shores and heading south to West Palm, but I'm not interested in dragging July's dead body downtown. Instead, I head east until we hit the beach road and then crawl along that while July stares out the window.

Truthfully, our destination isn't as important as how the journey is even possible. I want to be the type of person who's capable of accepting that his ex–best friend has risen from death and who can make the most of however long they have together, but that's not how I'm wired.

"Cut it out," July says, and I don't know what she's talking about until she eyes my fingers thumping the steering wheel.

"Sorry." I still my hands. "Look, I'm trying real hard not to freak out, but I'm seriously freaking out."

"Is it helping?"

"No."

"Then stop."

It's a good thing I'm driving, because it forces me to focus on the road and the cars in front of me and my foot on the gas pedal so that I don't lose it on July. "Maybe you can ignore what's going on, but I can't."

July tugs on the seatbelt and shifts the angle of her body toward me. "I thought you were the expert at ignoring things."

"You're dead, July."

"I'm *not* dead!"

"The smell of you decomposing is filling my mom's car." I pause and wait for July to argue, but she doesn't. "You might be able to walk and talk and annoy me, but you are still a rotting corpse, so please stop trying to change the subject."

July cranks up the stereo, which is connected to my phone and is still on the playlist I'd chosen earlier. The manic beats behind the auto-tuned voices dance from the speakers. It's a song called "Last First Love," and the overwrought lyrics about a broken heart don't match the upbeat tempo. I quickly turn it down.

"Were you listening to—"

"Yeah."

"For real?"

"Yes!" I say. "My ex–best friend died, and I was saying good-bye to her, and I put on some music that reminded me of her. Is that so surprising?"

"Of *me*," July says. "You were saying good-bye *to me*. The songs reminded you *of me*."

I open my mouth to agree with her, but stop and change course. "No. July Cooper died. I don't know who or what you are."

"Well, I don't know who you are either. The Dino DeLuca I knew wasn't such a prick." July barrels along before I can get a word in. "You keep saying I'm dead, but I don't feel dead. I don't feel like I'm rotting. I feel alive. Mostly. Maybe. But that's not the point. The point is that if anyone gets to be freaked out by this, it's me!"

July doesn't intimidate me. I mean, okay, dead July is a little scarier than live July had been, because I'm not sure if this version has superstrength or is contagious or is going to grow razor-sharp fangs, but I'm not bothered by her yelling the way some people are. I once saw her reduce a freshman to tears for forgetting his lines during dress rehearsal for *Into the Woods*. I know July, though, and she's all bark and no bite.

At least, I hope she doesn't bite.

I park the car on the side of the road. "Then let's talk about it. How do you think this happened? Why did it happen? Do you remember anything about being dead?"

"Stop assuming I was dead," she says.

"And . . . what? The paramedics who came to your house, the coroner who pronounced you dead, the medical examiner who performed your autopsy, and my parents were too stupid to notice that you were alive?"

July shrugs. "You said it, not me."

I choose to ignore that. "You had to have done something."

"Why do you figure it's gotta be my fault?" July asks. "How could I resurrect myself if I was dead?"

"You think I'm responsible?"

July holds up her hands. "Sorry, I forgot. You're never responsible for anything."

"I take the blame for my mistakes," I say.

"Like how you totally owned up to broadcasting to anyone who'd listen that I did it with Manny Silvas?"

I sputter while I try to think of what she's talking about, and then I remember. "First, that was months ago. Second, I didn't do that. If I was going to start a rumor about you having sex with someone, it wouldn't have been with a guy as hot as Manny."

"Ew! Manny's a creep!"

"A ridiculously hot creep."

July can't argue with that because, while Manny is a dick who thrives on making other people's lives miserable, he's so damn pretty. "Well, if you didn't spread it around, who did?"

"Probably Manny," I say. "The same way he told everyone sophomore year that he got a hand job from Mrs. Kaufman."

July rolls her eyes. "Yeah, but no one believed that."

I spread my hands. "So Manny learned from his mistakes."

"But they believed I did it with him? Why? Because I'm such a big slut?"

"You're not a slut, July. Even if you had slept with him, it wouldn't make you a slut." I wait a second to give her a chance to breathe, and then I remember that she doesn't need to. "My point is that I didn't do it, and you've been mad at me about it for months. Maybe there are other things you're pissed off at me for that aren't my fault."

July's face softens, but then it goes hard again almost instantly. "And maybe there are things you *did* do that I'm not pissed off about but should be."

I groan and slam my fist on the steering wheel. "Can we please focus on why you're undead?"

"I'm *not* dead. But you're making me wish I were."

"Me too," I mutter. "You can't keep denying the truth. You might not be dead, but you're not alive either. This could last another hour or a year or forever, and we need to figure it out so we can decide what to do with you."

"Who cares?" July asks. "I'm alive or not-dead or whatever right now. I don't know why. Could be a strange quirk of science or that I was exposed to some new radiation. Or it could be that the Ghost of Friendships Past saw deep down in your charcoal heart that what you wanted most was one last night with me."

I cough "Doubtful," but July ignores me.

"You can tell me I'm dead until the words lose their meaning, but it won't change that I'm not, and I don't want to waste the time I have."

The thing is, I can't argue with her logic. The nerd in me that needs to understand everything is dying to drive July to a lab and cut off pieces of her to look at under a microscope to see if I can figure out what's keeping her alive, and the poet in me wants to ask her a million questions about being dead so that I can understand how she sees the world and what the stars look like through eyes that once saw what's on the other side of life. But July doesn't need a nerd or a poet. She needs a friend, and I suppose that unenviable job has fallen to me.

"Then tell me, July. What do you want?"

"To go home," she says. "I want to go home?"

JULY

DINO THINKS HE'S BEING SUBTLE WHEN HE ROLLS DOWN the window, so I smack him in the arm. Maybe I don't know much—I don't know why I woke up in the DeLuca's chop shop; I don't know why I can't feel my heart beating; I don't know what happened after I blacked out at home; I don't even know if I'm dead or alive or not-dead—but I do know I don't smell. July Cooper is *not* the smelly girl.

I live in a subdevelopment called Liberation Dunes, which is stupid seeing as there are no dunes and it definitely isn't liberated. All the houses are painted one of seven approved colors and each is landscaped using the same selection of native Florida plants and bushes. The first time Momma and Daddy brought me and Jo here to show us—this was before the divorce—I said it reminded me of the scene from *A Wrinkle in Time* where Meg winds up in that neighborhood with the identical houses and the cloned kids bouncing the same red ball. But we've been here six years now, so it's home whether I like it or not.

Dino drives past the house, loops around at the end of the road, and parks in front of the sidewalk near enough so that we can see the house but far enough that the shadows do a decent job hiding us. His phone keeps buzzing in his pocket and he keeps mashing the buttons to quiet it.

"No one's home," I say.

"How do you know?"

I'm getting tired of having to argue with Dino. Used to be that I could tell him something and he'd accept it. "Because Momma's been refinishing furniture in the garage, so she's had to park in the driveway. No car in the driveway means no one's home."

"Jo could be there."

I point at the upstairs window, which is dark. "You see her light on?" The only light on is the one in the foyer that shines through the bay windows in front of the stairs.

"Fine," Dino says. "No one's home. Now what?"

No use in answering. If he doesn't know why I'm here, explaining it won't make a difference. I open the car door and head out, leaving Dino to either stay or follow, though I'm betting he's too spineless to leave the safety of the car.

I jog across the cul-de-sac toward the house. It's one of the smaller houses in the neighborhood, but it still feels huge the way it looms across the night sky, its shadow spilling over me. I head around the side and get the key out of the ceramic turtle in the backyard and use it to let myself in.

The house smells like Momma, which means it smells like food. During the summer it's fresh fruit and grilled veggies and meats. Chicken soup when someone's sick, chocolate and fudge during Christmas, chili when Momma's in the mood for it. More than the perfume she's been wearing since before I was born or the coconut conditioner she uses or even the faint hint of weed she smokes to treat her anxiety that she thinks she's so good at hiding; it's the million scents of home-cooked food that remind me of her.

The thing is, walking through the door and smelling what's cooking always felt like coming home. But this time is different. I recognize the furniture and the foods, but I feel like I've broken into a stranger's house. Everything is off, like it's on the verge of spoiling.

I catch the breakfast nook out of the corner of my eye. The table I was sitting at; the chair I must've fallen—Nope. Not doing this. Trying to remember what happened that night is a whirlpool of emotions that I won't allow myself to get trapped in. I run upstairs to my room.

My phone. I grab it from where I left it charging on my desk. I turn on the flashlight. Nothing's changed. Not one single molecule has been moved. Bed's still made, Xbox controllers are still on the floor, comic books are still stacked on my nightstand. I wonder how long Momma would've left it like this. Would she have turned it into a shrine? Let the dust grow thick over my stuff, or would she have waited a couple of months and then converted it into a meditation room or let Jo use it to store her growing collection of trophies and awards? Even if Momma hadn't been willing to touch my room, there are a million belongings of mine Joëlle coveted, so it was only a matter of time before she would've broken down and started taking what she wanted.

But I'm home now, so it doesn't matter. I'll sit in my room and wait for Momma and Jo. They'll be happy to see me and Daddy can come over and we can be a family again. For a while. Eventually, they'll ask the same questions as Dino. They'll need to know what's happening to me and how long it's going to last. And what if it doesn't last? What if I die tomorrow or in a year? Just when they've gotten used to the miracle of my return, they'll be forced to face losing me a second time.

I start to tremble. If I had tears, I'd be bawling. But I can't do this. I won't do it. Because I'm not dead. Or not-dead. If I were dead, I wouldn't be here. And if I went from dead to not-dead, maybe I can go from not-dead to alive. Or maybe I'll die again. Either way, I'm not going to sit here and wallow in what-ifs and maybes.

I should change and return Dee's clothes. It feels good to slip into my own jeans and to get out of that hoodie and put on a thin black blouse with a high enough neck to cover the incisions. I even trade the shoes I borrowed from Delilah for a nice pair of sandals. I rifle through my closet for a bag to stuff Dee's clothes in, and spot this coral dress that I love. Momma saw it on sale and bought it because she said she couldn't imagine anyone but me wearing it. Tags are still on it. I stuff it into the bag too.

What am I doing? What was I thinking? I can't stay here. I've only been dead for four days and not-dead for four hours and this already feels like not-home. I've got to get out of here. At least until I'm confident this is going to last and that I won't be subjecting my parents and Jo to more heartache. I refuse to let them get their hopes up if this isn't forever.

As I turn to leave, a rumbling rolls from the floor to my feet and legs. It's the garage door. I am so screwed.

DINO

WITHOUT WARNING, JULY OPENS THE CAR DOOR AND BOLTS.

"Wait! Where are you going?"

But she doesn't answer. She's out of the car before I can stop her, slamming the door shut and sprinting across the street. What the hell am I supposed to do? If I chase her, we could both get caught. And what if she's wrong and her mom and sister *are* home? July knows her family better than I do, so if she says they aren't home then I have to believe her, but she's not infallible.

Instead of worrying, I keep trying to figure out what's happening. July may not want to understand, but I do. I refuse to believe there's not an explanation for her condition. There are drugs and toxins that can make people appear to be dead by slowing their heart rate and breathing to negligible levels, but I doubt that's what happened to July. She had an autopsy. The medical examiner cut her open and removed her internal organs and weighed them and recorded them. He even took out her brain, though in July's case that might be an improvement. The point is that in the extraordinarily unlikely case she wasn't dead before the autopsy, she certainly would have been by the end of it. I guess it's possible that there's some unknown biological agent at work. I've read about a fungus that invades an ant's nervous system and controls it. That could be happening. Maybe.

If I can't explain it with science, that leaves the realm of miracles. I'm not sure where I stand on religion, but I do believe there are wonders that defy logic. This could be one of them. But if an omnipotent deity exists and is capable of raising July from the dead—mostly—why would they? It certainly couldn't be so we could argue about our failed friendship. If there's a god granting miracles, why didn't he help restore Puerto Rico's power and get them clean water after our stupid president failed to? Why didn't he stop the angry men with guns? Why didn't he eliminate the garbage from the oceans or wink the nuclear weapons out of existence? July was my best friend, and even though I'm confused about how I feel, there is part of me that's happy she's not-dead. And yet, it still seems like a waste of a miracle.

I'm so caught up thinking about July that I nearly miss Mrs. Cooper's car as it drives past, turns into the cul-de-sac, and pulls into the driveway. The garage door begins to rise and the outside flood lights trip on. I slide low in my seat, watching as Mrs. Cooper and Joëlle get out of the car.

"Oh shit," I whisper.

I have no way of sending a message to July, and she's going to be trapped inside with them.

Then I see her. July. Her face pressed against the upstairs window, waving her arms frantically. I'm too far to see her expression, but I can imagine her wide-eyed terror as she realizes her predicament.

I jump out of the car and trot toward Mrs. Cooper and Joëlle. They see me and freeze, confused—it's late and I have no reason to be here—but I have to give July time to escape.

"Dino?" Mrs. Cooper says. She stands in front of the garage, which actually is full of old furniture, with her keys in her hand. I didn't even know Mrs. Cooper had started doing restorations. Last I heard she was working on her next novel.

"Hey." I shove my hands in my pockets and try to look as bereaved as possible.

Mrs. Cooper offers me a smile, but there's an emptiness in her eyes. A hollowed-out darkness. "Dino, what're you doing here?"

I didn't plan beyond running from the car, and now I'm panicking. I don't know how much time July needs to get out of the house, so I stall for as long as I can.

"I was out driving," I say. "My feet brought me here. Or, wheels, I guess."

Joëlle huddles close to her mother and watches me wordlessly. She looks like there's a density at the center of her that's pulling everything toward it. Devouring who she is. Mrs. Cooper rests her arm around Jo's shoulders. "Do you want to come in, Dino?"

"No!"

Mrs. Cooper sighs and frowns. "I know this is tough for you—"

"I'm sorry," I say. "I shouldn't have come. I don't know why I came. It's just, July. I miss July."

The looks on their faces. I feel awful doing this to them. Bringing up July. Using my grief as a distraction. There's a special room in hell being prepared for me right now. I hope this is worth it.

Mrs. Cooper moves toward me. "Dino—"

"Good . . . Good night," I say. "I'll see you at the . . . I'll see you tomorrow." I walk quickly to my car. They're still standing in their driveway watching me, so I crank the engine and crawl away.

Jesus, she knows. Mrs. Cooper has to know. Okay, maybe she doesn't know July is not-dead, but she has to suspect something's up.

I watch the clock. I wait until two whole minutes have passed, and then shut off my lights and slowly reverse down the street until I'm in front of July's house. The floods are dark and the garage door closed.

Did July make it out? A burst of pain hits me in the bladder and I can't tell whether I'm going to puke or piss myself, and then a shadow detaches from the side of the house and dashes toward the car, arms flailing. It's July, it has to be. She might as well be screaming like a banshee.

July opens the door and throws a bag onto the floor and herself into the seat and yells, "Go, go, go!"

I put the car in drive and floor it, the momentum helping slam the door shut. July's laughing her ass off by the time we reach the top of her development, and I park and round on her.

"What the hell were you thinking?"

July grins. "That I didn't want to run around wearing Dee's clothes." Her new outfit suits her more, but it wasn't worth the risk. Then July pulls a coral dress out of the bag. She beams at it like she's going to be wearing it while strutting down the red carpet.

"You risked being caught so you could get a dress?" I ask. "Where the hell are you even planning to wear it?"

"Wherever I damn well feel like it."

I'd strangle her if she weren't not-dead. "Since I'm guessing you won't let me take you back, where to now?"

July looks at me with an evil grin that makes my heart stutter and skip a beat. She licks her lips slowly and says, "You know? I've changed my mind. I think I'm getting hungry after all."

JULY

HECTOR LOOKS ME UP AND DOWN AND TUTS. "GIRL, YOU need some sun."

"She's dead," Dino says.

I elbow him in the ribs. "*Not*-dead."

The bitter-apple expression on his face doesn't change. "And is that smell coming from one of you?" He wrinkles his nose. "It smells like death and regret."

"I don't know why you're both looking at me," I say. "Maybe one of the toilets is clogged. Besides, it's not like this place usually offers up a bouquet of wonderful aromas." I glance meaningfully at the kitchen. "Now, are you gonna seat us or harass us all night, Hector?"

He clicks his tongue. "No need to get feisty." Then he leads us to a table as far from the other customers as possible. "Coffee?" he asks, but doesn't wait for an answer before sashaying away.

"When you said you were hungry," Dino says, "I thought you meant for good food."

Monty's is a hidden treasure that's sort of like the queer child of a Waffle House and a Cracker Barrel, and it's a favorite of late-night club kids, strippers, and drag queens, though it's way too early for that crowd.

"Remember when we found this place?"

A smile brightens Dino's face, bringing out his cute dimples. "You got us lost trying to find that coffee house where they were doing the slam poetry contest and—"

"I did not get us lost!"

"You were driving."

"And you were navigating," I say. "Your only job was to repeat what your phone told you."

"I did," he counters. "But someone gave me the wrong address. Broadway and North Broadway are two totally different streets."

Hector returns with a couple of mugs of dark liquid that resembles coffee. He's got narrow shoulders, a round waist, and eyebrows peaked like Everest. "Haven't seen y'all in a while."

"Been busy," Dino says.

He wags his finger at Dino. "Hush, boy. I didn't mean you; I see you more than I see my own mother." He raises an eyebrow at me. "How come I don't see you no more?"

"Because Dino got a boyfriend and new friends and didn't want me cock blocking him." I catch Dino scowling out of the corner of my eye, and good. Let him be pissed.

Hector smirks. "The friends are rowdy and don't tip nearly well enough, but the boyfriend's cute."

"Wouldn't know," I say. "Never met him." Hector and I simultaneously turn our judgmental spotlights onto Dino and watch him wither under our harsh glares.

"Well that don't mean you can't come in and see me."

"I will," I say.

Hector pauses a moment, then says, "You hungry or extra hungry?"

"Extra hungry."

He nods. "Food'll be out eventually. Angie's on the grill, but the girl showed up stoned and is pretending we're too stupid to notice, *and* she's been fighting with her boyfriend on the phone since she showed up, so . . ." And then he wanders off to take care of his other tables.

"I missed this place," I say. "And Hector too." The carpet's a mottled brown, probably to camouflage roaches skittering from one side of the diner to the other; the vinyl booths are cracking; there's not enough bleach in the state of Florida to clean the stains from the tables; and the rest of the decor is straight 1980s, but I think it's the only place in the entire world where I could walk in wearing a gold sequin gown, a studded leather corset, or a hoodie looking dead, and no one would judge me. Except Hector, but he judges everyone.

"You know I brought Ruby here once," I say, "but she saw one little smudge on her water glass and ran out the door."

There's a hardness in Dino's eyes that I missed before. A

harsh glint in the dark blue that I can't read, which is surprising because I used to be able to read all of Dino's moods. But then it disappears; no, more like it tries to hide and make me think it's gone. "What'd you expect?" he asks. "I don't think she's been to a restaurant that doesn't have a full-time sommelier in her entire life."

"Look at you and your fancy words."

"It's your fancy word, not—" Dino stops and suddenly becomes intensely interested in the table.

"You're still reading *The Breakup Protection Program*?"

Dino nods, then says, "Well, for a while. I quit when you ruined the story." Even though I might have returned from the dead—though I'm not conceding that everyone who touched my body was a moron who missed the signs that I was not, in fact, dead—Dino's revelation might be the biggest surprise of the night. *The Breakup Protection Program* is a sprawling soapy story about two best friends who start a business in high school to help couples end their relationships without any drama, which obviously creates twice the drama. I've been writing and posting it online since the summer after freshman year.

"You said the writing was shit," I say. "You said it was a shit book with shit characters and that I was a shit writer who shouldn't be allowed to write a to-do list."

Red creeps up Dino's neck, spills into his cheeks, and climbs to the tips of his ears. "I never said that."

"Whatever you say, *ElevensiesForever*."

"That's not my screen name."

"Maybe not your regular one," I say. "But you're the only person I know writing *Doctor Who* and *Stranger Things* crossover fan fiction."

"Hey," he says. "There are at least ten of us."

I lace my fingers together and fold them on the table. "Do you deny that you left the comment? You can tell me. I won't be mad."

Whatever. I don't need Dino to confirm what I already know, but I enjoy seeing him squirm. Part of the problem with the anonymity of the Internet is that every troll with a keyboard can spew whatever nonsense he wants without repercussions. If everyone was forced to face the person they were attacking, they might choose their words more carefully.

"Fine, yes, I said it."

I lean across the table and punch Dino in the arm as hard as I can, which is pretty damn hard.

"Ow! You said you wouldn't be mad!"

"That wasn't anger," I say. "That was the mighty fist of consequence."

Dino rubs his arm, glowering. "I'm not the only one who thinks the new chapters suck. First, you have Aimee and Zach get together, which is ridiculous. They're best friends and they built the program as a team, and there's no way in hell they'd ruin their friendship with a doomed romantic relationship. But then, since you'd already screwed it up beyond repair, you had them break up and use the program on each other."

I wait for the boy to take a breath—it's like he's got

super-lungs now that he's tearing apart my work—but he finally reaches the end of his rant, giving me the chance to cut in. "You could've said that. It's a hell of a lot more constructive than the comment you actually left."

Hector arrives with a tray full of food. I guess there are some folks who order off the menu, but doing so is dangerous. What's good depends on who's cooking, and usually the special is whatever's about to spoil that they need to get rid of. Letting Hector order for us ensures we won't wind up with *E. coli.*

Tonight he drops off two omelets stuffed with peppers and cheese and topped with sour cream; French toast; and two slices of what I think are blueberry cobbler.

I lean my face over my plate and suck in air through my nose, which feels weird. Breathing's not supposed to feel so strange. The aromas of the eggs and cheese and sour cream mingle together, but they don't quite smell right. They're off somehow.

"At least tell me Aimee and Zach make up. I don't care if they're friends or more, but they can't walk away from one another." Dino speaks in a voice that's nearly a whisper.

"You'll have to wait for the rest of the book like everyone else." Only half my mind is listening to Dino. The rest is trying to figure out why this food smells wrong.

"Me and your other tens of readers?"

"Hey, I have over a thousand readers, thank you very much."

"Well, if you were planning on finishing it before you died, you've failed."

"Not dead." I stab the eggs with my fork and pull the omelet apart to let the insides spill out. A cloud of steam bursts up, but it stinks even worse. "Does your food smell right?"

Dino sniffs his meal and then nods. "It's fine to me. Why?"

"You know how milk gets that funk when it's a couple days past the expiration date? Not spoiled but not great either. Like, you'd use it for cereal but you wouldn't drink it straight?"

"Yeah."

"That's how this smells." I bring the French toast closer to try it, too, but it's the same.

Dino takes a bite of his eggs. "Tastes fine too." But he's frowning and staring at me and I don't like that I can't read him.

"What?"

"I was wondering how you were planning to eat."

"With my mouth? Like a normal person?"

"You don't have a stomach," he says. "Whatever you swallow is going to fall into your chest cavity."

"You don't know what you're talking about."

"When are you going to face reality? You aren't breathing, you look dead even buried under layers of makeup, your heart isn't beating, though I'm not convinced you had one to begin with, and if anything's sour at this table, it's you."

"Ha-ha."

"Fine," Dino says. "Keep pretending you're a real girl."

I cut off a corner of French toast, swirl it across the plate until it's good and soaked in butter and syrup, and stuff it into my mouth. Oh my God. It tastes like vomit that's been stewing in the hot summer sun for days. Like Angie blended maggots and month-old fish together and threw it on the griddle. But the worst part is that Dino's staring at me, watching with a self-satisfied grin, and I can practically hear him chanting *Told you so, told you so, I was right, I told you so.*

"Well?" he asks.

"It's good." But before I finish the words, I spit the chewed food onto my plate and then scrape every last particle from my tongue with a napkin.

Dino gags. "Hector's going to be so thrilled when he clears the table." He pushes his plate away.

I grab a fresh napkin and lay it over the spit-out food like a shroud. "What the hell is wrong with me?" I immediately look up and point at Dino. "And don't tell me I'm dead."

"No clue," he says, his voice streaked with sympathy.

"How am I supposed to return to my life if I can't even eat like a normal person?"

"Maybe you're not." Dino tries to nibble some bacon without being obvious about it. "I get that you're afraid to face the truth, but you don't have a choice. You might not be dead, but you're not alive either. Based on the smell, you *are* still decomposing. If this state you're in isn't permanent, we have no idea how long it's going to last; and if it is? We need answers, July. We have to understand what's happening to you before we can decide what to do with you."

I laugh bitterly. "We? Last time I checked, we weren't a 'we' anymore."

"Despite what you think, you can't do this alone. And I'm not letting a corpse my family is legally responsible for run around the county unsupervised."

"You're not worried about me," I say. "You only care that I don't bankrupt your parents' business."

"That's not true."

"Stupid July ruins everything. That's why you never introduced me to Rafi, isn't it? Afraid I'd screw that up for you too."

Dino goes quiet, which is fine by me. He can't make the food not taste like hot pus, so he's basically useless. And what does he even know? He puts makeup on corpses; he's not an expert on everything death related. But maybe he does have a point about figuring out what's happening. I want to go home, but I can't give Momma and Daddy and Jo hope if there's a chance that this isn't for real. They won't care if I rot and shrivel, so long as we're together, but I care.

"You called Rafi my girlfriend."

"What?" I'm too busy mourning my taste buds to care about listening to Dino, and only partly hear him.

"I'd been dating Rafi for a week, and we were at your house watching a movie, and you asked when you were going to get to meet my girlfriend." Dino looks up at me through his lashes.

"So what?"

Dino's jaw twitches and one of his eyes gets wider than the other. "So what?"

"Yeah," I say. "I call you my girlfriend all the time. If it was a problem, you should have spoken up."

"I didn't think I had to."

"It was a joke! I was joking!"

"But it's different with me, July. Rafi's trans, you know that, and I doubt he would've laughed."

"Rafi this and Rafi that, and forget everyone who isn't him."

"I'd have been pissed about you saying it even if I wasn't with Rafi, but I was—"

I raise my eyebrows. "Was?"

"Am! I am with Rafi."

"Wait, is that why you stopped talking to me?"

"No," Dino says. "That's why I stopped inviting you to hang out with us. You were the one who stopped talking to me. Besides, don't act like you didn't cancel every time I tried to arrange for the three of us to spend time together."

Dino's phone buzzes in his pocket, and he grabs it and mutes it, mashing that button as hard as he can.

"Any reason you've been ignoring those texts? Are they from him?"

"Rafi's having a party, and he wants me to go."

The idea of a party sounds wonderful. Loud music so I don't have to listen to Dino, and lots of people so that I can lose him for a while. "Let's go, then."

"Not happening."

But I'm not taking no for an answer. "I'm sorry about the joke. It was dumb and I should have realized it was wrong and apologized, but we can go and no one will have to know I'm me. Since Rafi and your friends never met me, and they don't go to our school, you can tell them I'm a cousin in town for Delilah's wedding."

"No!" Dino says it so loudly that it catches Hector's attention from the other side of the diner.

"Then what the hell good is being not-dead?" I say. "I can't see anyone, I can't eat, I can't go to a stupid party. If I have to spend the rest of my not-life with you, I'd rather be dead again!" I get up and storm out of the diner.

DINO

I FINISH MY FRENCH TOAST. JULY'S WALKING CIRCLES IN the parking lot, and Hector's watching me from across the diner, but I continue eating like my life isn't a garbage fire wrapped in a disaster. Except then Rafi texts me again, and I glance at it and see the messages he's left. Mostly they're pictures. Selfies of Rafi with Shanika in the kitchen. Pictures of everyone in the pool. More selfies, this time of Rafi with his dog, Dobby.

RAFI: miss u!

RAFI: leon and charlie have been screaming at each other over whos the best power ranger all night

RAFI: so i figure theyre definitely gonna be a thing by morning

RAFI: you okay

RAFI: i know you said not to ask but im worried
RAFI: ♥ u

I'm not surprised about Leon and Charlie. Anyone who didn't see that coming from miles off wasn't paying attention. And Rafi's dog honestly does look like he's one raggedy sock away from earning his freedom. It's the last message that's got me twisted. Is he trying to emoji his way into saying he loves me? That is the last distraction I need tonight.

I pay the bill, say good-bye to Hector, and leave.

"About damn time!" July says when I reach the car, where she's sitting on the trunk with her arms crossed. I guess one upside to being not-dead is that she can't sweat and ruin her makeup. I've barely been outside for ten seconds and drops are already beading on my forehead and running down my spine. "When someone takes off, you're supposed to follow them."

Getting that last text from Rafi unbalanced me, and I snap at July without thinking. "Maybe I'm tired of chasing you. Did you ever think of that?"

July slides off the car and gets in my face. "What does that even mean?"

This is usually when I stand down, but not tonight, Satan. "This is our pattern," I say. "You say something awful, we fight, you run off, and then I have to track you down and apologize when I'm not the one who screwed up!"

"You screw up plenty."

"Remember sophomore year when you 'borrowed' my biology

midterm take-home? And then lost it?" My hands are flying as I speak, and in the back of my mind I realize I've become my mother, but I have to file that realization away until I can process it later. "You didn't lose yours, of course, and I had to grovel to Mr. Schwartz for a redo, which he gave me but only after penalizing me a whole letter grade."

July flares her nostrils and backs off a little. "I remember. So?"

The defensiveness in her tone annoys me even more. "So I was justifiably angry, and you pulled your pissy vanishing act. Only, that time I decided that I wasn't going to chase you. I was going to wait to see if you came to me. You didn't. For a week. You cost me an A in biology, and yet, in the end, I was the one who apologized."

"Cry me a river, build a bridge, and get over it."

"I got over the test a long time ago," I say. "And now I'm over being the one who always has to apologize. Christ, July! You died before coming to me to fix our friendship so that you didn't have to say you were sorry."

A scraggly man wearing way too many layers for the Florida summer stumbles between me and July on his way toward the road.

"Excuse you," July says. But the way he's weaving makes me pretty certain he's not in the mindset to care. I kind of envy him.

When he's moved past us, July rounds on me. "First of all: I've got nothing to apologize for, so if that's what you're waiting on, you can keep on waiting if it gets you off, but you're going to be disappointed. Second: You think you're the one who has to chase me? I crawled back from the dead for you!"

I motion at July and say, "I don't know why *this* is happening, but I'd believe you returned from the dead for a slice of cake before I'd believe you returned for me."

July's eyes fly wide. "Fuck you, Dino." She storms off toward the road and stops at the sidewalk.

When I catch up to her, I say, "I'm sorry."

July's quiet for a moment. Then she says, "I'm not ashamed of loving cake."

"I know."

The anger I felt in Monty's evaporates, unlike the layer of sweat coating my arms and face and chest. Maybe it doesn't matter who chases whom so long as the friendship survives. The trouble is that I'm not certain ours should. TV makes it seem like the majority of friendships die in fiery explosions of anger and recrimination, but my experience has been that most friendships simply fade. Chris Sanchez was my best friend in fifth grade. I don't have a single memory of that year without him in it. And then sixth grade came and we weren't friends anymore. We didn't have a fight; we were still in the same class together. But the ephemeral ties that had bound us together for that year had disappeared. Maybe July and I hadn't actually been Best Friends Forever. Maybe we'd only been Best Friends Until Someone Better Comes Along.

"I think Rafi told me he loves me," I say. It's a random change of subject, but we've nothing left to gain by arguing over who should do the chasing during a fight, and I can't shake it from my mind. "He wrote 'heart u,' which isn't the same as 'love you,' but it's a baby step toward saying it. And I don't know if he does. Or if I do. What if he says it and I don't reciprocate?"

This is the longest I think July's gone without interrupting me, so I nudge her. "July? You listening?"

"Hush!" she says, and points across the street. Jog is a busy six-lane road during the day, and it's even worse at night. The drunk guy from before is staggering in the median looking like he's going to try to cross.

"Stop!" July yells. The man stumbles into the road. A tan truck blares its horn and swerves, barely missing him, but the man looks like he has no idea what's going on. "We've got to help him." July tugs at my arm, but I pull her away from the road to wait for a gap to open. We dodge the cars and run across to the median, but now the man is in the middle of the street, cars weaving around him.

"Get out of the street, moron!" I call, but he's still acting like he can't hear me, so he's either pretending or is completely smashed.

"I'm going after him," July says. I grab her arm before she can run into the road and cause a crash. "Let me go!"

The man stumbles. He doesn't see the accident about to happen. But I do. It's a tricked-out Honda with an aftermarket exhaust screaming through the night, heading straight for the man. And the driver doesn't look like he's going to swerve. I yell and July cries out and the Honda's driver finally crushes the brakes, but it's too late. The tires squeal and the brake pads burn, but it's too damn late. The car slams into the man, who doesn't even see it coming, and he smashes into the windshield and flies across the hood. July tries to bury her face in my chest, but I disentangle myself from her and run toward the body—because surely he's a body now and not a man. There's no way anyone could have survived that.

The driver is barely older than me, and he's out of his car crying that he didn't see the guy and why was he in the road and going on about how it isn't his fault. The man is half on the sidewalk, face up. His neck is turned at an impossible angle and his right arm is twisted and his right leg is bent and he's bleeding from somewhere. From everywhere. The driver tries to move the man out of the road, but I yell at him not to.

An hour passes in a second. Other people stop to help. One of them is a nurse. Paramedics and police arrive. The medics take over the drunk guy's care, the police take my statement. It's a blur, and then they're gone. They're gone, and I'm in the parking lot of Monty's with July, who wisely disappeared before the police saw her.

"You okay?"

I think I am. And then July rests her hand on my neck, and I'm bent over throwing up in the bushes. Everything comes out.

I stand, and July hands me a napkin and a bottled water, and I don't ask where she got them from. I'm just so grateful I can rinse out my mouth.

"Now I'm okay," I say.

"First time seeing a dead body that fresh?" July asks. She adds a fake chuckle, and I know she's not actually so cruel as to joke at a time like this and is only attempting to get my mind off what happened.

I spit and then say, "He wasn't dead."

A crease forms between July's eyes as she frowns. "There's no way he survived."

Everything feels like waking up from a dream so real that I can't tell if this is reality. The lights seem harsher, the air hotter. Even July's voice sounds sharper and yet distant at the same time. "He should have died," I say. "His neck was broken. That's what the medic said."

"Then how—"

"I don't know. She told me she's been seeing it all night. People who should be dead but aren't. No one's dying." I look into July's blue eyes because she's also supposed to be dead but isn't.

July takes me by the arm and guides me to the passenger side of the car.

"What're you doing?"

"We should go," July says. "And I'm driving."

"I can drive."

"Doubtful." She glances at my hands. They're trembling and I can't stop them, so I give her the keys.

July takes a minute to adjust the seat and the mirrors and get familiar with where the lights are.

"Do you know what it means if people stop dying?" I ask.

"Your parents quit pressuring you to join the family business?"

"I'm being serious."

"I guarantee death hasn't stopped."

"Says the girl who was dead yesterday." It was one level of weird when it was only July. Yes, it freaked me out and I wanted to understand why it was happening, but it was an isolated event that I could sort of pretend was a miracle to keep from losing my mind. But if death is suspended somehow? How do I deal with that? It's too much for my brain to process. Compared to that, July returning to life is hardly an issue.

July starts the engine and puts it in reverse, but she keeps her foot on the break. "Hey," she says.

"Yeah?"

"Remember the concert I took you to for your birthday?"

I nod. "Strange Attractors. Best concert ever."

"I got the money to buy those tickets by selling your bio midterm to Justin Blake." She pauses. "Sorry."

JULY

I NEVER DROVE LIKE A GRANDMA UNTIL I SAW SOMEONE get plowed into by a speeding car. I should be shaking. My brain should be flooding my body with adrenaline or whatever chemicals it spews out during a crisis, but it's not. Add freaking out to the list of things I can't do since I woke up at DeLuca and Son's. Alive, not-dead, or whatever the hell I am, I still can't get the accident out of my mind. I should have tried harder to reach the guy. Assuming for a nanosecond that Dino's remotely right, it wouldn't have mattered if I'd been hit by a car. If I'm dead, I can't get deader. But what if I broke some bones? Would those knit back together?

No. It's pointless thinking about this because I'm not dead. I may not have the answers, but I know "July's dead" isn't one of them.

Dino's phone is blowing up, and he's texting replies furiously. "Rafi?"

"My mom."

"You need to go home?"

He shakes his head. "She's checking on me and reminding me that your funeral is tomorrow—like I could forget—and telling me that she's set my suit out."

"Oh."

I don't know where to go, so I drive on muscle memory and we wind up at Walmart, which is where we used to go after Monty's, seeing as it was the only place open near Palm Shores late at night. Dino gives me a curious look, and I shrug.

"You got a better idea?"

"No," he says. "It just seems like we should be trying to work out why you're a walking corpse, not killing time at Walmart."

"Where should we go, Dino? To the shadowy secret science base at the edge of town that doesn't exist because this isn't a movie and some helpful dweeb isn't going to come along and enlighten us about our situation with a lengthy expository monologue seconds before he tragically dies a meaningless but horribly graphic death?"

Dino frowns. "I was thinking more like the cops or to talk to my sister, but Walmart's fine."

The upside about Walmart in the middle of the night is that everyone kind of looks dead, so I blend in. We stroll up and down each and every aisle and manage to go ten whole minutes without arguing or freaking out, which is nice.

"Hey," Dino says. "Did you know they have a water bottle with a filter built in?"

I turn around and he's standing in the middle of the aisle pointing at the bottle, wearing a shit-eating grin. "No way!" I say, and we both crack up.

"Remember the first time you saw that thing?" Dino says.

"It was cool!"

"It's a water bottle."

"With a filter built in!"

Dino's smile grows. "No? For real? Tell me more!"

For one second, all is forgotten. All is forgiven. We're a couple of friends going on about something that no one else in the world would understand. I might have been a little over-enthusiastic the first time I saw the bottle, and every time we went to Walmart after that, Dino made certain to point it out to me. It's stupid, right? But that, and a million other stupid things, are the threads of a friendship. They're the threads of my friendship with Dino.

And then he's gotta ruin it by talking.

"We should go back to your house."

The smile and laughter and the good feelings vanish. "Why?"

"To tell your mom you're still alive."

"So now I'm alive? Make up your mind."

"You're something," he says. "Don't you think your parents deserve to know?"

"Are you serious?" Is he serious? I search his eyes, I check the size of his nostrils and the angle of his head for some sign that he's messing with me, but he's not.

He stuffs his hands in his pockets and walks to the end of the magic water bottle aisle and turns down the next, leaving me to chase him, which I make a mental note of to remember the next time he says he's the one always doing the chasing.

"Dino?"

"Tell me this is real." Dino looks at the items on the shelves and the ceiling and his hands held out in front of him. And at me. He looks directly at me, and there's a moment where I'm not sure he sees *me*. Like I'm not a person anymore but a burden he's carrying.

"What?" I ask. "You think maybe my death hit you so hard that it sent you into some kind of dissociative state and that you're actually in a psychiatric hospital, drugged and drooling, instead of at Walmart with your best friend who, until a few hours ago, you believed was dead?"

"I wouldn't have put it like that."

I snort. "This is real. It's happening."

Dino's chin dips to his chest like that's what he feared. "You're not-dead," he says. "Other people aren't dying—"

"Allegedly," I say. "According to one paramedic."

"Still, this is a thing that's happening. It's not a Christmas miracle—"

"Because it's the middle of summer?"

"July . . ."

"What?"

"Don't you *want* to tell your mom and Joëlle that you're alive?"

An older woman rolls around the corner in her motorized

cart and glares at us like she was expecting to have the entire store to herself. I grab Dino's hand and drag him toward the toy aisle, which is where we used to spend most of our time. I liked the action figures, and Dino couldn't help buying LEGOs. When we're clear of anyone who might be listening, I turn to him.

"Why do you think I went home before? Clothes?"

"Kinda."

It takes all my strength not to smack him. "I was sitting in my room planning to stay there until Momma and Jo came home, but then I started wondering how long this is going to last." I close my eyes and wish I could breathe so that I could suck in a lungful of air and let it out and feel the relief that comes from it, but I can't. "You think I'm avoiding what's happening, but the truth is that I have to keep moving or the reality of my situation will crush me. You want answers? I want them too! But I have no idea where to start, and I'm not going to give my folks hope until I know it's real."

Dino rakes his hand through his hair, pulling it off his face. "I understand that; I really do, but we can't wander aimlessly and hope we stumble on the answers. Your funeral is tomorrow. Your parents are expecting to see your body in a casket. To bury you. We have to tell them or you have to go through with the funeral."

"Maybe I will," I say.

"Don't be stupid." He keeps shaking his head like he can rattle the bad thoughts of out it, but if it were possible I would've done it long ago.

I wander down the aisle and stop in front of the Star Wars toys. Dino's shadow falls over me as he shuffles nearer.

"What if I'm the cause?" I say.

"Of?"

"This. Me. Of that drunk guy not dying."

Dino cocks his head to the side. "You think, rather than you being not-dead because something's stopped people from dying, that people have stopped dying because you're not dead?"

"You got a better explanation?"

Him losing it laughing isn't the reaction I expect. I've never understood how such a deep, soothing voice could come out of a scarecrow body like his, but his rich laugh carries down the aisle and across the store, and I'm guessing they can hear it in the grocery section. "What?"

Dino bends over with his hands on his knees to catch his breath. His face is splotchy red, and there are even tears running down his cheeks.

"What the hell is so funny?" I ask again.

"You," he says. "Death might have been suspended, and you've made it about you."

I flare my nostrils and stare at him. "You seen any other zombies?"

"No. But it's typical. Everything's about July Cooper."

"Is not."

Dino straightens up. "Clearly you've forgotten about when I came out."

I resist the urge to roll my eyes. "How could I forget when you made such a big deal about it?"

"When I told my parents I was gay, my mom started leaving condoms in my sock drawer, I couldn't watch a single TV show with my dad without him asking if I thought whatever guy on-screen was cute, and Dee baked me a chocolate cake and wrote 'Not a surprise' on it."

"So?"

"When I told you, you cried. You decided you'd turned me gay on account of the time in eighth grade we practiced kissing on each other."

"That's only because Wesley Sato had just come out, like, a month before, and I'd kissed him too!"

Dino goes on like he's not listening. "And then, after I consoled you and convinced you that you didn't cause my raging case of homosexuality, you made it your mission to tell everyone at school."

"I was proud of you!"

"You stood up in the middle of American history and announced that I liked boys and that anyone who messed with me would face your wrath."

"Once again," I say. "So?"

Dino taps his fingers on his thigh and stares at me with nothing but anger. He's always been the type of person to hold things in, but there's fury in there that looks like it's been simmering for longer than we've been friends. It's cold and dark, and I didn't know he was capable of it.

"Forget it," he says, and starts to turn away.

"Forget it, my ass!" I say, which stops him. "You think I'm the one who makes everything about them?"

"Me?" he says, all innocent.

I nod furiously. "Hell, look at tonight. I'm the one who's not-dead, but you're acting like you should get to make the decisions. Where we go, what we do. Trying to force me to see my parents. The truth is, you don't know how long this will last. I could be dead again by morning, and you won't even let me go to a stupid party to meet your stupid boyfriend and your stupid friends. Are you ashamed of me? Is that why you won't let me meet them?"

"No, July."

"Then why don't we go see *your* parents?"

"Fine! Let's!"

"I was being sarcastic."

Dino scrubs his face with his hands. "Why is this happening to me?"

"To you?" I say, incredulously. "Whatever you think, Dino, this isn't your story; it's mine. I may die at the end, but I'm still the hero and you ain't even the villain. You're nothing but a pathetic unnamed background character who doesn't make it out of the second act."

I dig the keys out of my pocket and dangle them in the air in front of him. "We're going somewhere," I say.

"Yeah," he says. "To your house or mine."

I try to make a buzzing sound, but it comes out more like a dry fart. "Wrong answer."

Dino plants his hands on his hips and puffs out his bottom lip. "I'm not taking you to Rafi's party."

I shrug. "Fine. Then I'll go without you."

DINO

"YOU DON'T EVEN KNOW WHERE RAFI LIVES!" I CALL AS
July takes off. She thinks I'm going to chase her again, but I'm
not. This is merely one more example of July indulging in her
flair for the dramatic. I'll hang out in here for another ten minutes, and then I'll go to the parking lot where I'll find her waiting
by the car for an apology, which she isn't going to get.

I asked my mom when I was younger how people could go
on once someone they loved had died. I didn't comprehend
how they could make decisions and talk about funeral plots
and coffins and the ridiculous but necessary minutiae involved
in burying a body that lacked the capacity to care anymore. I
could've asked my dad, but people don't make sense to him
until they're dead. My mom, though, she understands the
living, and she explained that we each have an amazing ability to rationalize and compartmentalize. Either we convince

ourselves of facts and truths that don't necessarily line up, or we box reality up and hide it in some distant corner of our minds like a bomb on a timer we'll be forced to confront one way or another.

I've been dealing with July's not-death by rationalizing it. Since the moment July sat up and screamed, I've been attempting, and failing, to piece together an explanation out of the limited facts at my disposal. I want to believe that there is a scientific and totally logical explanation for July, but in the absence of science, I'm willing to accept that this could be the result of a religious miracle. Pick a religion, any religion. I'm open minded. Of course, the possibility that other people may not be dying has complicated matters greatly, but I'm still confident we will find an answer, be it rational or divine.

July, however, seems to be compartmentalizing. She's bent on pretending this is normal, that tonight is merely a random adventure shared by two ex–best friends ambling about town, dragging up the corpses of their past mistakes. I'm not certain she's accepted that she's not actually alive. I've witnessed July in denial before, but this isn't like the time she refused to admit she couldn't pull off a perm. July's refusal to face reality doesn't change that her funeral is tomorrow. In the morning, my mom or Delilah is going to open the freezer in the office expecting to find July's body. They're going to dress her and prepare her to Mr. and Mrs. Cooper's specifications. Then they're going to arrange July inside the coffin the Coopers selected, load it into the hearse, and deliver it to St. Mark's Catholic Church for the service, after which we'll drive to the cemetery and bury July in a six-foot-deep hole.

Actually, it's more likely that, unless we explain what's happening to our parents, Mom or Delilah will find July missing from the freezer, they'll call the cops, the Coopers will freak out—and who could blame them? Dealing with the theft of their daughter's corpse?—my parents will lose their business and the house, and we'll have to move to a town in a state where no one knows us. Someplace like New Amsterdam, Indiana. Either way, ignoring our situation won't change what's coming, and I need to make July see that.

I guess it's been long enough, so I walk to the parking lot. "You've got to be kidding me." My mom's car isn't there. There aren't enough cars for it to be hiding, but I keep looking anyway, like it's the fridge at home and if I close and open the door enough times, food that wasn't there last time will have magically appeared. But the car isn't going to suddenly materialize. July actually left, and I have no way to contact her. This can't be happening.

I walk to the front of the store and sit on a bench beside the exit. Every time a light flashes in the lot, my head jerks up expecting it to be July. It isn't.

"You all right?"

I didn't notice the woman standing in the shadows against the wall. She's wearing a blue vest with a tag on it that says her name is Ruby, and she's smoking.

"Sure," I say. "Why wouldn't I be okay?"

Ruby takes a drag and blows the smoke away from me, but the wind carries it in my direction anyway. "'Cause you look a little rough." She steps out of the shadows and sits beside me. She's younger than I thought. Maybe not much older than me. A bit of ink peeks up from the edge of her collar on the side of her neck, and I wonder what it is.

"My best friend died—ex–best friend . . ."

"Damn. I'm so sorry."

I brush her sympathy off. "It's fine. She came back to life, which you'd think would be cool, but we've been fighting all night. And then some guy got run over, but he didn't die—and why not? Apparently no one's dying—and I only wanted to talk about it and figure things out, but she's selfish and stubborn and abandoned me to teach me a lesson."

Ruby fidgets with the cigarette between her fingers. "The dead best friend?"

"Ex."

"Whatever."

"The whole situation is ridiculous. I'm not the one who needs the lesson; she is. This is her fault. Leave it to July to ruin dying, and not just for herself; for everyone." I rake my hair with my hands. "I can't believe this is happening. I'd go home, leave her to sort out this mess herself, but, oh yeah, she stole my car."

Ruby raises her eyebrows and then flicks her cigarette away. "Dude, just call an Uber." She gets up and walks toward the entrance doors.

"Thanks!" I yell. "Great advice! Why I didn't think of that?"

"Asshole," she mutters before going in.

I can't sit in front of Walmart all night, so I pull out my phone. Two more missed texts from Rafi. Neither contain hearts. He'd pick me up if I asked him, but then I'd have to explain why I'm here and where my car went, and I wouldn't know where to begin. Calling my mom or dad or Delilah presents the same set of problems. Damn, maybe Ruby was right and I should call an Uber.

No. I can't go home without July. I pull up Rafi's messages again. The last one was a picture of the pizzas he'd ordered. The one before that a weird almost-haiku about beer. My thumbs hover over the letters. What do I say? *Hey, I need your help. It involves a talking corpse. It's better if you don't ask questions.* Probably not the best idea. Rafi's amazing, so I could tell him the truth and he'd believe me—or he'd pretend to believe me—and would help me in any way he could. But no. I can't do that to him. I can't drag him into this mess. It wouldn't be fair to him or to July.

Finally, I decide to walk. My house is only a couple of miles away, and maybe July will realize how wrong she was and turn around and see me walking and feel horrible that she made me exercise and sweat. Nah, that probably won't happen.

When I'm about halfway home, I pass the strip mall with the Taco Bell, which is open, and the Publix, which isn't, and I spot my mom's car parked at the edge of the lot. *Thank you, Jesus!* But as I walk, I spy someone with weirdly big hair get out of a truck, jog toward my car, and start pounding on the windows. And they're yelling July's name.

JULY

"YOU DON'T EVEN KNOW WHERE RAFI LIVES!" DINO
yells across the store, but the joke's on him. I'm not going to his
stupid boyfriend's house.

Dino's an idiot. I bet he's still in the store thinking if he stalls
a while, he'll come out and find me waiting for him like a good
little July. That boy's gonna be surprised when I'm gone.

Problem is I don't know where to go. I get in the car and crank
the engine and put it in drive and then idle for a minute. I'm not
going home—mine or Dino's—but I've got to go somewhere, so
I pull out of the lot, turn right, and drive.

This is so easy for Dino, isn't it? Telling me to show up at my
house looking like death and surprise my mom with my new
situation. I know exactly how that would go. She'd scream and
then cry. She'd hug me and drag me inside and spend the next
few hours trying to feed me. At some point Jo would wander

downstairs and my dad would come over, and we'd celebrate like me being not-dead was some kind of miracle.

Guess what, though? This ain't no miracle. A miracle would be if I'd opened my eyes in the chop shop without these disgusting cuts across my chest or with the top of my skull attached to my head by actual skin instead of stitches. If I could finish the musical I've spent most of my summer rehearsing for or start my senior year and graduate or find some ugly dress to wear to prom, which I'd end up going to with Benji 'cause he'd be the only person who asked.

The miracle would be getting my life back. And I want that. I want it more than I've wanted anything, and that includes seeing my name at the top of the *Paradox Legion* leaderboards, though making those gamer assholes who give me grief see my name up there would be pretty sweet too. No, I want my life back more. And I'd take it if I knew I could keep it. That's what Dino doesn't get. This isn't living; it's waiting. Waiting for whoever raised me to change their mind and take it away again.

I look up and see 7-Eleven and cut a hard turn and pull into the parking lot. I check myself in the mirror and it isn't pretty. My hair's lost its shine, and while the makeup's keeping me from looking gray and dead, it also makes me look flat. Not much I can do about it, though. I dig through Dino's car and come up with a five-dollar bill and about three more bucks in change.

The inside of the convenience store is harsh yellow, and the woman behind the register barely looks at me. I walk straight for the Slurpee machine, grab the biggest cup, stick it under the blue-flavor nozzle, and pull the lever.

Nothing happens.

I pull again.

"Come on!" I try the Coke flavor, which is a seriously inferior Slurpee flavor, but not so much as a drop drips from it either. I stand and watch the motor spin inside the machine. "I know you've got Slurpee in you. Give it up!"

I pull the lever so hard that the entire machine and the cups and lids on the counter shake and rattle.

"Is there a problem?" calls the woman from the counter. Her thick eyebrows are dipping to her nose.

"The machine's full of Slurpee, but it's not working. I want a goddamn Slurpee!"

The woman sighs with weary resignation. Like she's accepted that this store is hell and that her punishment is to spend eternity helping hapless idiots like me. Her dirty-blond hair is tied in a ponytail that hangs past her waist, and a charm bracelet dangles on her wrist, making tinkling sounds as she walks. When she reaches me, she gives me a hard stare but then shoos me out of the way.

"I already tried that," I say as she holds a cup under the nozzle and pulls the handle. She glares in response.

After a minute, she pulls off the panel in the front and looks underneath. "How bad would it scuttle your night if I slapped an 'out of order' sign on the front and left this for the day crew to fix?"

"My best friend Dino—except he's not my best friend anymore; he hasn't been for a year and I'm starting to wonder if he ever was—and I used to have a gaming night every Friday."

"Role playing?"

"Video."

The woman turns up her nose.

"Before either of us had a car, I'd bike from my house and he'd bike from his and we'd meet in the middle. Here. Load up on snacks—"

"And let me guess," the woman says. "Slurpees."

"Exactly!"

I don't know how many Friday nights we spent slurping Slurpees and flying spaceships, but there's a whole chunk of my life that feels like it was forever. That I was born playing games with Dino and that we would die playing games together.

The woman grabs a wad of napkins from the condiment station next to the hot dogs and wipes grease off her fingers. "If he's not your friend anymore, why do you need a Slurpee tonight?"

Nostalgia had drawn me here, but I don't know why it's so important that I get a Slurpee. Judging by what happened at Monty's, it's not like I'll be able to drink it without wanting to puke, which I assume I'm also incapable of. But then the idea that's been brewing in the corner of my mind bursts forward.

"It's for him," I say. "My friend. We've been hanging out tonight for the first time in a year, but mostly we've been fighting, and I want us to be okay but I don't know how to get there. I'm hoping a Slurpee will help."

"Sure, whatever," she says. "But is there any way I can convince you to get your reconciliation Slurpee elsewhere?"

"Please," I say. "I need this. I didn't realize how much I needed it until right now. Bringing Dino a Slurpee will remind him of those Friday nights lying on the floor in his room or mine, shooting enemy ships, talking about everything and nothing, wondering what our futures were gonna to look like." I laugh to myself. "There was this time for, like, three months when Dino was convinced he was gonna be a filmmaker, so he recorded everything on his phone and tried making a movie out of it, but I fell asleep while he was showing it and he got so pissed."

The woman breaks in and says, "This is thrilling, but seriously, if you can fix your problems with a Slurpee, you can probably fix them without one."

Ding!

Someone comes into the store. The woman sighs again and returns to her post, leaving the question of whether or not she's going to fix the machine unanswered. I need to go pick up Dino, but now that I've got it in my head that I want these Slurpees, I don't want to go back without them, and the woman is being mighty unhelpful.

Out of the corner of my eye, I catch sight of the girl that came in as she heads to the drink cooler. She's humming a familiar tune, so I take a quick peek. Frumpy skirt, glasses, brown bouffant. *Oh shit!* Zora Hood.

I drop to a crouch and duck walk to the edge of the aisle so that I can glance around the corner. She must be on her way home from *Hairspray* rehearsals. That's why I recognized her humming. She's my understudy for the summer show at Truman High that I'm in. Was in. Whatever. She opens the cooler door and pulls out a couple of root beers, then stops at the chips and grabs two bags before heading to the counter. I've got to get out of here.

While the cashier is ringing her up, I creep toward the door, sneaking along the back end of the aisles to avoid walking near Zora. I'm clear. I'm going to make it. I open the door and then I hear, "July?"

For not even half a second, I freeze. Barely noticeable, right? She couldn't have seen me pause, which was hardly classifiable as a reaction.

"July Cooper?"

But, of course, she did. I speed up, digging my keys from my pocket. I get into the car and start the engine and reverse out of the lot as quickly as I can. Zora runs out of the store as I'm pulling away. If my heart hadn't been cut out and stuffed into a plastic bag before being shoved back into my body, it would be beating so damn hard right now.

What the hell was I thinking? How would I have explained to Zora Hood why I, a girl who died a week ago, was in a 7-Eleven trying to buy a Slurpee? This is why Dino didn't want me to leave the funeral home. He feared something like this would happen. It nearly did. What if that had been my dad? He doesn't live far from here. He could've gotten a craving for beef jerky or a burrito and decided to run to the corner store and seen me and then everything would've been a mess. Maybe the best course of action is to pick up Dino and drive to his house and hide until I know how long this is going to last so that I don't get into trouble.

I stop at a red light to make a U-turn, and Zora pulls up beside me in her dad's pickup truck. Her windows are down and she's yelling, "July? Is that you?"

Thank goodness my windows are tinted, but why won't this light change?

"Roll down your window!" she yells.

I ignore her. That's my only option. Ignore her and hope she goes away.

The light changes to green, finally, and I floor it, pulling a U-turn and heading toward Walmart. I glance in my rearview and spot Zora behind me. She always was too persistent for her own good. Nice enough, but she didn't know when to back off. And now I have no idea what to do. Obviously, I need to lose her—I can't bring her to Dino and get him in trouble—but I'm not sure how.

There! A Taco Bell, and there's a cop car in the lot. I cut into the turn lane, wait for a gap in traffic, and pull into the lot. I park far enough away to avoid too many people but near enough that I'm visible to the police cruiser. Then I kill the engine, lock the doors, crawl into the back seat, crouch down on the floor, and wait.

It's less than a minute before Zora is knocking on the windows and calling my name. My plan, which isn't honestly much of one, is to hope that the cop will come out of Taco Bell, happy and full of chalupas and sour cream and hot sauce, see some random girl freaking out around the car, come to investigate, hear Zora explain how she thinks she saw a girl who's supposed to be dead driving a car, and arrest her for obviously being on lots of drugs. It's horrible, but it's all I've got.

"July? I swear to God I saw you. Come on! Open the car!"

"Hey," a second voice says. "Is there a problem?" At first I think it's the cop, but no. I know that voice. It's Dino.

DINO

WHEN I WAS THIRTEEN, I CAME HOME FROM SCHOOL, went into the house and got a snack, and then walked across the lawn to the office. I opened the door and found Dad standing in the center of the room in an apron that said YOUR OPINION WASN'T IN THE RECIPE, singing that awful song from Titanic, while Mom was sitting at the desk—atop which rested a severed arm—crying. I turned right around and left, and to this day I still have no idea what I walked in on.

Finding Zora Hood pounding on the window of my car in a Taco Bell parking lot while shouting July's name produces about the same level of confusion. The major difference being that I can't walk away this time.

"Hey, Zora. What's going on?"

I've known Zora on and off since middle school, and we were both in theater together with July. She's the kind of person who drifts through different groups but never sticks with one for long. Basically the M&Ms of school acquaintances; neither particularly exciting nor objectionable.

"Dino?" Zora's breathing heavily and her olive cheeks are speckled pink. "Where'd you come from?"

"Taco Bell," I say, so that I don't have to explain why I'd walked from Walmart. "What're you doing to my car?"

Zora adjusts her glasses and squints. "Your car?"

"My mom's, officially," I say. "But she hates driving, so I use it more than she does."

"Then why was July Cooper driving it?"

I cross my arms over my chest. "Not cool. You know July's dead. It hasn't even been a week."

"I'm serious!" Zora's voice rises into its upper range. "She was at 7-Eleven and I caught her reflection in the door's glass and I was like, 'Hey! That looks like July Cooper.'" Her glasses fog up and she pulls them off and cleans them with the hem of her blouse. "So then I followed her down Military and stopped at a light and it *was* her! She made a U-turn and I caught up to her here."

I have so many questions. Not that I can ask the person who may have the answers seeing as I have no idea what's going on or if she's even in the car.

July's the actress, not me, but I do my best to look skeptical. "Nothing you said is even remotely possible." I hold up my hand and cut Zora off before she can jump in. "First of all, this is my car. I drove it here so I could enjoy a burrito. I parked it here, where it's been the entire time. Second, July Cooper is dead.

Want to guess how I know? Because her body is in the freezer in the mortuary less than fifty feet from my house."

Zora rests her hands on her hips. "I know what I saw."

Motion behind Zora catches my attention, and I glance up to see a Palm Shores police officer exiting Taco Bell and walking toward his cruiser. Zora sees me looking and turns.

"Good," Zora says. "He'll settle this." She waves the officer down. "Excuse me! Officer, sir?"

The cop stops, looks, sighs heavily, and then trudges toward us. He's wearing the look of a man who just finished a bunch of tacos and wants only to find a quiet place to park his cruiser and take a quick nap. Instead, he gets us. His name tag reads RODRIGUEZ.

"Problem?"

Before Zora can take control of the situation, I leap to answer. "Sorry, sir. I came out of the restaurant and this girl was pounding on my window, and I want to go home but she won't let me leave."

"That's not true!" Zora says, her voice reaching dangerously high.

Office Rodriguez barely hides the eye roll. "Why don't you tell me what's going on."

"Yeah," I say. "Tell him how you claim you chased this car, which has been in the lot for at least an hour, down Military and that the driver was a girl who died last week."

"It was!" Zora says. "Her name's July Cooper, and she was driving!"

"Are you sure this girl is actually dead?"

I nod. "Look, Officer, I don't know why Zora's doing this—she goes to my school, but I don't know her well—but the girl she's talking about? She was my best friend and her funeral is tomorrow and none of this is funny. I just want to go home."

Officer Rodriguez looks from me to Zora. "Wait here a minute." He motions at Zora and leads her off to the side.

"I hope this was worth it," I whisper. If July heard me, she doesn't reply.

Zora talking emphatically, pointing at the car, and Rodriguez keeps calmly telling her to slow down. My phone buzzes and I pull it out. Another text from Rafi. A few. I read the chain but the officer returns before I finish.

"You can go," he says. "My condolences about your friend."

A flood of relief rushes through me at those words. I was terrified he was going to call my parents and they were going to show up and everyone was going to find July in the car, and then I'd have to explain why, and my life as I know it would be over forever seeing as, dead or alive, July's still a corpse.

I turn to open the door but—duh!—it's locked.

"Problem?" Officer Rodriguez asks.

"Forgot to unlock it," I say loudly, hoping July gets the message. I reach into my pocket where my keys would normally be and pretend to press the unlock fob. The locks click and the lights flash and I could kiss July if I didn't also want to shove her out of a speeding car into the middle of the interstate.

"Drive safely," the officer says, and heads toward Zora.

July's hand pokes up from between the seats and shoves the keys at me. As quickly as I can, I start the car and leave. July stays hidden, and I don't speak. When I'm sure we're far enough from Taco Bell, I turn down a side road, stop in front of Belvedere Park, and get out of the car, slamming the door behind me.

I'm sitting on the wood fence when July approaches.

"Thanks—" she starts, but I cut her off.

"Do you know how that felt?" I ask. "I just gaslighted Zora Hood. The best-case scenario is that the cop lets her go home and Zora spends the next ten years in therapy trying to convince herself that she didn't actually see you at 7-Eleven!"

"I know but—"

"Worst case is that he humiliates Zora by calling her parents and making them pick her up. Either way, I lied to her and a cop in order to convince Zora that the truth isn't true, all to save your ass!" My lip is quivering, and my whole body is shaking.

July clenches her fists and squares her shoulders. "So what? She deserves it."

"No one deserves that." My face twists in disgust. I know she doesn't have a heart, but I didn't know she was heartless.

"Then take me back," she says. "Or give me the keys and let me go alone. I'll admit to the officer that Zora was telling the truth about seeing me. That I died and returned and stole your car so that I could go to 7-Eleven."

The way she's standing, I believe she's serious. And I'm almost willing to let her. This situation is so out of my control, but letting July go wouldn't make anything better. It'd only drag me and my family into it.

"You're not going."

July grabs for the keys, but I pull them out of her reach. "Give 'em here!"

"Stop it!"

But she doesn't. She reaches past me to get them and I lean away to keep them from her, but I lose my balance and topple backward. July slips and falls on top of me, and not even that stops her. She wrestles for the keys, and I go to grab her hand, but something comes off between my fingers.

"What the hell was that?" I scramble for my phone and turn on the flashlight.

"Oh, fuck!" July's holding up her right hand, and her thumb is all muscle and sinew. And cradled in my hand is the skin, slipped off like a glove.

"Gross!" I toss the skin at her and crab walk backward.

July picks up the skin and tries to slide it on, but it looks loose and wrinkled. She keeps trying, but when it's clear it's not going to stay on, her entire body deflates. Well, not really. It's actually likely that she's already filling with gases that are going to have to escape sometime, and I'm hoping it's not while we're together.

I climb over the fence and pop the car trunk. I dig around in my mom's roadside apocalypse kit, which is a lot like a regular emergency kit except that it also contains powdered coffee, a couple of MREs, and a few other things one might need if their car broke down at the end of the world.

July's still sitting in the grass when I return. "Here," I say, and toss her a tiny tube of superglue, and then sit across from her. "Spread it on your thumb and then slide the skin back on."

I watch while July struggles to position it straight. The ragged edges where it tore look horrible, but she smears some glue there too. I have no idea how I'm going to explain that to my parents when they prepare July's body for the funeral.

"What did you mean before when you said Zora deserved it? I thought you were friends."

The more July fiddles with her thumb, the worse it looks, but it's no use telling her that. "We are. She's my understudy."

"So?"

"Did you see her hair?" July asks. "That was Tracy hair. Which means she's already stepped into my role. Mine. Do you know how long I've been dying to play Tracy Turnblad?"

"Since forever," I say, which is true. *Hairspray* is July's favorite musical, but she could never get Mrs. Larsen to stage it at our school, so she auditioned for the summer program at Truman High, which is open to all students, when she learned they were putting it on, which I know thanks to Benji.

"Exactly! And now Zora's going to ruin it with her annoying voice and her skinny, waifish ass."

"Crapping on someone for being thin isn't any better than crapping on them for being chubby."

July lets out a frustrated sigh. "I know, I know."

"Then stop doing it."

July doesn't respond, but I said what I needed to. I doubt it will make her stop, but hopefully it'll make her think before the next time she calls me a skeleton. Besides, her anger at Zora makes sense now.

"You gonna get your phone?" July asks.

I didn't even notice it buzzing, but I mute it. "It's only Rafi. Again."

"What does he want?"

"He wants me to come over. He's having an issue with one of our friends and he wants me there to help him."

July's face perks up. "Then let's go."

"We've been through this. Your skin is literally falling off. Don't you think it's time we talked about what to do with you?"

"I'm a person, Dino. I decide what to do with me."

"I didn't mean—"

"No one cares what you meant." July holds out her thumb, though it's tough to see it in the dark. "This doesn't prove I'm dead. It could have happened to anyone."

"Anyone dead," I mumble.

"What're you scared of? I promise I won't embarrass you."

My phone vibrates, and I know what it says without needing to look at it. Rafi is almost as persistent as July when he wants to be. "Fine," I say. "But we're only staying for a few minutes."

"Deal."

"And after, we *are* going to discuss what's happening to you and decide what to do."

"Maybe," July says, and I know it's the best I'm going to get.

I let out a long sigh. "Well, I guess you'll finally get to meet Rafi. But first, we have to make a stop."

JULY

DINO THROWS ANOTHER SHIRT ON THE FLOOR AND stands in front of his closet in a pair of dark jeans that hang off his hips. "This is impossible."

"Then pick a lame outfit, and let's go." I was surprised when Dino told me we needed to run by his house so he could change. For someone who's spent the whole night saying how much he didn't want to go to this party, he's acting like it's prom.

Dino kicks off the jeans and pulls on a pair of preppy gray shorts and throws a black-and-white short-sleeve hoodie on. "I can't go looking like a slob." He ducks into the bathroom connected to his room and tries to tame his hair.

"Since when did you start caring how you look?"

He doesn't answer, and it's okay. I already know. It was when he started dating Rafi and hanging out with the other kids from the community center. Right around the time he and I stopped being friends. While the water's running, I sit at Dino's desk and pop open his laptop. Being someone's best friend means never going through the photos on their phone without asking first, and never looking at their browser history. But, as he loves pointing out, we're not best friends anymore. I'll try not to judge him too harshly.

The boy spends way too much time on the Internet. Not that I'm judging. Definitely not judging that. Or that. Nope. Not me. But then I find what I'm looking for. He lied when he told me he'd quit reading *The Breakup Protection Program*. Based on his history, he's been checking it for updates three or four times a day, even after my supposed death. The water shuts off, and I slam the laptop.

"What about me?" I ask. "Think I should change?"

Dino pokes his head out of the bathroom and looks at me. "Actually—"

"I was kidding."

"Oh."

A garment bag hangs off of Dino's closet door, and I unzip it and peek inside. It's a sleek black suit with a white shirt and black tie. This is what he was going to wear to my funeral. It's weird to even think those words. My funeral. I can't deny that I'm curious what that would have looked like, but it's not like I can attend as a spectator. Either way, Dino's right; I need answers so I can decide how to move forward.

"Earlier you were acting like you'd rather have your eyes poked with needles than go to Rafi's party," I say. "Don't you want to figure out why I'm not-dead or why no one else is dying or whatever?" Dino's open-mindedness to the weird, unexplainable bits of life is one of the things I've always admired about him.

Dino struts out of the bathroom. His wavy hair is wet and combed to the side, leaving a wide part that kind of looks like a bald spot. I'm not certain it's better than it was before, but we'll never escape this room if I tell him that.

"I'd rather have my toenails pulled out than go."

"What changed?"

"Why do you care?" he asks.

I shrug.

Dino sits on his bed while he pulls on socks and shoes. "It's Leon."

"Who's Leon?"

"One of Rafi's friends. Though I don't know if friend totally covers it. They're like siblings to him. He looks after them. Takes care of them. When Kandis's dad got out of jail and came home, Rafi convinced his parents to let her stay in the guest room. Only took a week for the guy to break parole and wind up back in prison."

Dino's saying these words, and while I recognize some of them, the rest don't make sense. Daddy loves *Star Trek: The Next Generation*, so I love it too, and I've seen every episode. There's this one called "Darmok" where Picard is trapped on a planet with this alien guy who speaks a language no one can understand. And it turns out the language is based on references to things. So, like, if I said, "Janet Jackson, at the Super Bowl," most folks would get that I'm referencing the unfairness of how after Justin Timberlake exposed Janet's nipple for millions to see, she was banned from performing there again while he was invited back.

Well, Dino and I were like that once. People who didn't know us could've snooped on our conversations, but they wouldn't have understood even a quarter of what we said. It's the kind of connection that forms when two people have known each other as long and as deeply as we have. Only now, the references have changed, and I barely understand him. In that episode of *Star Trek*, the inability to communicate leads to the death of the alien. I hope I can avoid the same fate.

"What does Kandis's dad have to do with Leo?"

"Leon," Dino says. "And nothing."

"Then why—"

Dino stops in the middle of tying his shoes and glances at me. "Context."

I make an O with my mouth.

"Anyway, Leon recently got over this breakup. For weeks it was an endless cycle of crying and Netflix and ice cream. He was a mess, but Rafi took care of him, which means *I* took care of him."

"Still not getting why it suddenly became imperative that we go to the party," I say. "And the more you explain, the less enticing you're making it sound."

"Not everything's about you." Dino finishes tying his shoes. "So back to the story. Gwen showed up at Rafi's with her new boyfriend who happens to be, you guessed it, Leon's ex-boyfriend. Leon's having a meltdown and Gwen's acting like—"

My upper lip curls. "Who are you?"

"What?"

"Last year, when Jack broke up with me to date some skinny girl with boy hips—"

"Didn't we just talk about that?"

"*Fine.* He dumped me for a girl with perfectly normal hips who's probably one of those people who believes the earth is as flat as your ass. My point is you gave me exactly one day to cry it out. One day. After that, every time I mentioned his name or looked like I was getting emotional, you'd roll your eyes and tell me to suck it up."

"We should go." He heads for the door.

"You've changed, Dino."

He pauses with his hand on the knob. "Look, we'll go to Rafi's, and I'll deal with the situation, and then we'll figure out what to do with you. Okay?"

"Fine," I say. "Whatever."

DINO

I DON'T KNOW WHETHER I'M MORE NERVOUS FOR JULY
to meet Rafi and the others or for them to meet July. Only, with
a little luck, no one will know they're meeting my ex–best friend.
It's too late to reconsider, though, since I've already texted Rafi
to let him know I'm on my way. I haven't told him I'm bringing a
guest yet, so that'll be a nice surprise.

"What name did you decide on?" I ask.

July's spent most of the ride touching up her makeup, ensur-
ing her skin is lively and even. "Roxane," she says. "I'm Dino's
cousin, in town from Knoxville for the wedding."

"Laying the southern accent on a little thick, don't you
think?"

"I don't tell you how to gay; don't tell me how to act."

I glance at her and frown. "How to gay?"

"Or whatever."

"See, comments like that are maybe why I never brought you to meet these people."

"You used to have a sense of humor."

No matter how hard I try to convince myself that this isn't going to end in disaster, I can't outrun the feeling that this is absolutely going to end in disaster. July's going to offend someone or more bits of her skin will slough off the way her thumb did. Taking her to Rafi's house isn't one of my better ideas. It's too great a risk. Yet here I am, turning down Rafi's street, parking on the road in front of his house, explaining the rules to July one last time.

"Don't talk to anyone unless you absolutely have to. In fact, try to avoid people altogether."

July rolls her eyes. "Maybe you'd feel better locking me in the trunk."

"That's not a bad idea."

"It's a terrible idea."

"Fine," I say. "But try not to act so much like—"

"Like what?"

"Like yourself." As soon as I say it, I wish I hadn't. We're here at Rafi's, and July and I were kind of getting along, and there's a much higher probability that she'll screw things up if she's angry at me.

"Do I even want to know what that means?"

"No."

"Dino!"

I flinch and say, "Fatima Jahani's Halloween party, sophomore year."

July's face contorts into an angry sneer. "You are *not* going to—"

"You pushed Anya into the pool! In her Gamora costume!"

"How many times do I have to tell you that that was an accident?"

"You're saying it wasn't a reaction to me giving her more attention than you?"

July mumbles under her breath, "I don't get what was so special about her anyway."

"She was new!" I yell. "I was trying to be nice."

July's face is a tight mask of anger and her body is giving off serious "go to hell" vibes. "You keep dredging up these horrible things I did, but if I was such a monster, why did you stay friends with me for so long?"

"Sometimes, I have no idea," I say. "Now, let's go do this, and if you could not cause a scene, that would be great."

"Depends," she mutters. "Does Rafi have a pool?"

Rafi lives about twenty minutes south of Palm Shores, in a historical preservation neighborhood. Rather than the cookie-cutter houses found in most of South Florida, the houses on Rafi's street are an odd marriage of Palm Beach eccentricity and Pueblo architectural design, built around the 1920s. His house consists of three multi-story cubes with soft, rounded corners at the top so that they kind of looked like adobe, but painted a garish flamingo pink, managing to be both culturally appropriative and tacky at the same time.

"Fancy," July says.

Cement steps are set into sandy-colored rocks that carve a

path through the lawn to the front door. The landscaping has the barely tamed look of a traditional English garden, with birds of paradise popping out from around a marlberry tree, bursting with white blooms.

My stomach is a swirling pit of sewage, and I feel like I'm trying to breathe from under a pallet of bricks. I don't know whether I'm this anxious because July's a walking, talking, rotting corpse or if I would have been like this introducing her to Rafi and the group while she was still alive-alive. Guess I missed my chance to find out.

When we're still ten feet from the door, it opens and Leon runs out, shoots past us, and darts down the street. Gwen trails behind, followed by Rafi, who grabs and stops her.

"Let me go!" Gwen says. She's tiny compared to Rafi, but she's got three rough older brothers, so she knows how to throw a punch.

"You're making it worse. Please go inside and let me handle it." Rafi's wearing blue medical scrubs for bottoms and a Hufflepuff house T-shirt. His hair is kind of messy, but on Rafi it totally looks charming and unplanned.

I cough, and both Rafi and Gwen finally notice we're standing here. Rafi's face explodes with a smile so bright it drowns out the rest of the world. With the power of that spotlight beaming at me, everything else is dark. Gwen stomps her foot, goes inside, and slams the door.

Rafi rushes me and kisses me, but I put my hand on his stomach and nudge him back.

"Don't stop on my account," July says. "I'm good to watch as long as the show's free."

I slide my hand down Rafi's arm and into his hand. "Rafi, this is Roxane."

"Roxy," she says.

"You didn't mention you were bringing a friend."

"Surprise," I say with mock enthusiasm.

July wisely keeps her hands buried in the front pocket of her hoodie. "I'm Dino's cousin, down for the wedding. From Knoxville. That's in Tennessee."

Rafi chuckles. "Thanks for the geography lesson."

"You got a nice house," she says. "Very . . . pink."

"Hideous, yeah?" Rafi says. "Dad's been fighting the historical society for years to paint it a different color, but we're not allowed."

July's eyes grow wide and she says, "Wow. That's super fascinating."

I can't tell if Rafi knows July is making fun of him, and the best I can do is give her angry eyes and send mental pictures of the many ways I'm going to torture her when we're done here, so I try to change the subject instead. "Hey, was that Leon who ran out of here?"

Rafi nods. "We did well keeping Leon and Adonis apart at first—"

"Adonis?" July asks.

"Leon's ex," I say. "And apparently Gwen's current."

"But then we started a game of *Fortune Street*—"

"Which is?" July asks.

This would go a lot quicker if July would stop asking questions, but I remember how confusing it was when I started dating Rafi and hanging out with his friends, so I say, "A sadistic version of Monopoly for the Nintendo Wii."

July shakes her head. "Monopoly isn't sadistic enough?"

"You have no idea," Rafi says. "It started fine. Leon was in first place but then Gwen rigged the market, sending Adonis into first place, and—"

"Leon flipped out?" I ask.

"He flipped the coffee table."

"Damn."

"And I should find him before he gets in trouble." Rafi squeezes my hand, and I feel both his and July's eyes on me at the same time; the weight of their expectations heavy and unyielding.

July sucks air through her teeth and then says, "Go find your friend. I'll mingle inside."

"I'm not so—" I begin, but Rafi cuts me off.

"There's pizza in the kitchen and drinks in the fridge. The liquor cabinet is off-limits, but you're welcome to the beer." And then he pulls me away before I can argue.

JULY

I WATCH RAFI AND DINO TAKE OFF. YEAH, OKAY. MOSTLY I watch Rafi. That boy is way too good looking for Dino. That ass in those scrubs, and the hair and that two-day stubble he's got going on? Damn.

I mean, *damn*. I might actually owe Dino an apology. If I was hooking up with a boy like that, I would've ditched me too.

Telling Dino to go with Rafi was easy. He likely thinks I did it so that he didn't have to choose between me and his boyfriend, but I really wanted the chance to meet his friends without him hovering over me. July might have embarrassed him, but I'm Roxy, and she's a class act.

Kidding. Roxy's the worst!

The inside of Rafi's house is as gaudy as the outside. The walls are painted weird pastels and there are family photos crowded on them, and every room has at least one bookshelf. Someone in this house loves to read. I peek into the living room and see that the party's moved outside to the patio. The shadows of Dino's friends are outlined by the lights from the pool, and bass from whatever music they're listening to is drifting in. I start to go out there so I can introduce myself, but with Dino and Rafi both gone, Roxy can't pass up the opportunity to do a little snooping.

After exploring a bathroom, an office, and what I think was Rafi's parents' bedroom, I finally find Rafi's room on the second floor. A person's bedroom is a microcosm of who they are. Take Dino's room, for example. He always throws his dirty laundry in the hamper but he never makes his bed, which says he likes order but isn't afraid to abandon it for expediency. The LEGO sets he keeps displayed say he's patient and loves building things, and isn't afraid to show that trait off, but that he also thrives on following directions, and doesn't do so well when he's got to improvise.

Now, let's see what psychobabble bullshit I can make up about Rafi.

Dirty clothes on the floor. Comic books on the floor. Computer parts on the floor. Seriously, does Rafi throw everything he owns on the floor? It's a minefield of worn boxer shorts and books and computer components and, oh God, that's a bowl of fried rice. I could never sleep in a room this disorganized. I'm not overreacting. It's like his closet and drawers regurgitated their contents onto the floor, and he's okay with it.

The miasma of foot funk and body spray is overwhelming and makes me consider retreating, but a photo on Rafi's desk catches my eye. I tiptoe through the minefield and grab the frame. The picture is of Dino and Rafi on what looks like some kind of nature trail. Dino's wearing a backward ball cap and Rafi's behind him, with his arms wrapped around Dino's chest. And Dino's smiling.

It's not that strange, right? Someone smiling for a picture? But Dino is practically allergic to photos. Over the course of our friendship, I tried everything to force him to smile for me. Out of the thousands of pictures I have of him, I can count on one hand the number where he's smiling a real smile. A genuine smile. Like the one in this picture of him and Rafi together.

I return the frame to the desk, which is covered with flyers for political rallies, notes reminding himself that he signed up to walk the beach at night to keep tourists from disturbing nesting sea turtles, pamphlets for the community center, condoms attached to informational tags discussing HIV and other sexually transmitted diseases, his schedule for school next year. He dances ballet? Dino never mentioned that.

"No," I whisper. "Don't even tell me." On his nightstand is a stack of printer paper. A manuscript. Rafi's a writer. I pick up a few pages and read them. The book is called *The Swarm* and what I read is violent and lyrical and brilliant. Damn. He's not a writer—he's a good writer.

Rafi Merza might be a slob, but he's also a saint who dances and writes. I assume he's going to cure cancer before he's eighteen and solve world hunger before he's twenty-one. It's no wonder Dino never wanted to introduce me to him. How could I have possibly compared? When we sold candy in school to raise money for theater, I ate the candy and then stole the money from Daddy's wallet to pay for it. The only time I ever picked up litter was in seventh grade when Mrs. Shelby made me clean the school parking lot because I said I'd rather pee blood than play dodgeball, which, to be fair, I ended up doing anyway after Marcy Kissinger nailed me in the kidney with the ball.

I never had a chance of competing with this guy.

Instead of finding scandalous dirt on Rafi that would prove Dino was wrong to ditch me, I've learned how much I don't measure up. Rafi's only flaw seems to be an inability to utilize drawers and closets for their designed purposes, whereas Dino's spent the majority of the night reminding me of my numerous inadequacies. I can't blame Dino for not wanting to introduce me to his boyfriend and friends. Compared to them, I'm a disappointment in every way.

Faced with this new information, July might have sat alone for the rest of night and moped or become belligerent and "accidentally" shoved someone into the pool, but I'm not that girl. Dino's new friends might not have liked July Cooper, but I'm going to make them *love* Roxane.

DINO

DID I REMEMBER TO PUT ON DEODORANT? IT'S HOT OUT and the sweat is already rolling down my crack and I don't want to stink, so I covertly sniff under my arm.

"You look adorable," I say. "Especially your Hufflepride."

"Leon!" Rafi calls. His bare feet slap on the ground.

"Any idea where he might have gone?"

Rafi nods. "There's a park this way. It's the only place in the neighborhood he knows."

"Why didn't you ask Gwen to leave?"

"I can't kick her out for dating a guy Leon used to date." He shakes his head. "The situation's messed up, and I'll talk to her about that later, but Leon's gotta grow up. Besides, if I have to avoid every guy Leon's dated, I won't be able to go to Barnes and Noble. Or Chipotle."

"The one on Congress or Military?"

"Both." He laughs, which sends a shiver up and down my arms. "And that doesn't even count that he treats dating boys who work at Starbucks like he's playing Pokémon."

"Gotta catch 'em all?"

"All he's gonna catch is herpes if he's not careful." Rafi kisses the top of my hand. "Hey, you." He smiles for me alone, and I melt.

"Hey."

I feel inadequate when I'm with Rafi. Like we're in a relay race and he's running with the baton, trying to pass it to me, but I can't run fast enough to reach it.

"Roxy seems decent," Rafi says.

"Sorry she's been keeping me busy tonight," I say. "She showed up unexpectedly, and I didn't know what to do with her."

Rafi looks at me curiously. "You didn't know she was coming for the wedding?"

"Dee 'forgot' to inform me I'd need to babysit."

"Either way, I hope she can handle Jamal," he says. "You know how he is. Has to know everything about everyone, and you've been the one mystery he hasn't been able to crack. The chance to grill a cousin about you? Irresist—"

"Why are you with me?" The question pops out before I can stop it. I've had my doubts, but spending the last few hours with July has amplified them to the point that I can't ignore them anymore. I'm scared of how Rafi might answer, but it's too late to turn back now.

Rafi starts coughing and stops walking, and I slap him on

the back until he holds up his hand to let me know he's okay. "Sorry," he says. "Choked on spit."

"How do you—"

"Do you honestly need to ask why I'm with you?"

His heavy brows knit together and dip down and he's looking at me like I asked him if the earth was flat or round. "Yes?"

Rafi rakes his hair with his fingers and whistles.

I squeeze his hand and tug him in the direction we were walking. "Forget it. It was stupid."

"No," he says. "But will you tell me why you want to know?"

I try to pull my thoughts together, but I'm not certain I even asked the right question.

"Maybe it's July," I say. "I've been thinking about her and why we stopped being friends. She did a lot of messed up stuff, but I think I did too. I know I'm not the best person, but I at least thought I was a good one. Now I wonder if even that's true. Then there's you. You're smart and kind and compassionate. You're dedicated to your future and to the people you care about. You know what you want to do with your life, and you work hard at it every day, never expecting anything to be handed to you. Plus, you're hot."

Rafi nods along like he gets it, which, I'm glad one of us does. "And you're wondering why someone as amazing as me is with someone like you."

"Kind of," I say. "I mean, look at what you're doing now. If July had freaked out and taken off, I would've let her go."

"Leon isn't July."

"How does that make a difference?"

Rafi sucks in a breath. "I'm telling you this because I trust you, okay?" I make a cross over my heart, and he nods. "When I first met Leon, he'd recently gotten out of the hospital."

"Suicide?"

"Eating disorder," he says. "So I worry about him when he gets upset." Rafi shrugs. "If Gwen had run off, I would have let her go knowing the worst she would've done was sit in her car and pound out her anger to one of the angry punk bands she loves. But Leon gets caught in his own head, so . . ."

"Oh."

We leave the well-lit sidewalk and cut into someone's yard, which butts up against a canal. Rafi doesn't seem concerned, and the grass is worn, so I assume this is a commonly used path to reach the park.

I'm getting accustomed to the quiet when Rafi says, "You're not a bad person."

I snort. "I'm indecisive, selfish, I keep my feelings bottled up until I explode—"

Rafi stops and takes my other hand and pulls me so that we're facing each other. "You think about your decisions from every possible angle, and you never let anyone rush you into making one; you are intensely protective of the people you care about most; you care about them so much that you're willing to sacrifice what you want to spare their feelings."

"That's not me," I say. "You've got me wrong."

Rafi slides his hand behind my neck and pulls me to him. He

kisses me, and I get lost for a second. I wrap my arms around him and he presses his body against me, and even though it's already so hot and humid outside, Rafi's warmth spreads from him to me, and I want more.

And then he pulls away and says, "I love you, Dino."

"I lo—" The words spring to my lips reflexively before my brain can process what my ears heard. "Wait, what?"

Rafi kisses my forehead. "And what's more is that you deserve to be loved."

JULY

I CAN'T DECIDE WHICH OF DINO'S FRIENDS I HATE MOST,
but Roxy loves each and every one of them. Dafne keeps trying
to get me alone to talk about video games; Jamal is ball light-
ning in a gangly human shape; Kandis hasn't said a single word
to me, but she's been quietly judging me since I walked onto the
patio; Gwen and Adonis are trying hard to look miserable but
can't hide their new-relationship glow; and Charlie, Shanika,
and Andy alternate between hanging out with us and playing
in the pool.

We're outside, relaxing in a sort of circle made of deck chairs.
A gentle breeze blows the smell of chloramines in from the pool,
and I'm idly petting Dobby, Rafi's scrappy, bug-eyed shelter dog.
Stupid adorable mutt's been following me around since I came
outside. Even though I don't know any of these people, the vibe

feels like one of my end-of-show cast parties. This isn't quite the same, but it's so normal and relaxing that I can almost forget the last few hours.

"Dino did that?" Jamal asks. It's question after question with him. I haven't decided if it's cute or annoying.

"Took a dive off the stage and gave himself a concussion," I say. "But he popped up and kept going. He doesn't remember much of it, which is for the best."

Everyone's laughing, and I even catch a smile from Kandis, but it disappears the moment she sees me looking.

Shanika, who's standing behind Gwen and Adonis, pretending she doesn't realize she's dripping water on them, says, "Never would've figured Dino for acting."

"For real," Jamal adds. "Sometimes it seems like the boy can barely play at being himself. Can't see him pretending to be someone else."

"He's not a good actor," I say. "But we needed more boys and I bullied him into it."

Kandis's eyes narrow, and she sits up a little straighter. "I heard his girl—" She snaps her fingers. "What's her name?"

"July," Dafne says.

"Yeah," says Kandis. "July. I heard she made him do acting."

Right. I did. Not Roxy. "Well, yeah," I say. "But Dino called to ask my advice, and I told him he should do it. I mean, what's the point of being gay if you're not going to be in theater?"

Eight sets of eyes turn on me at once.

"You're one of those, huh?" Jamal says.

"Stupid people from Tennessee?" I say, realizing I've done exactly what Dino expected me to do.

Jamal shakes his head. "One of those straight girls who talks about how much you love gays, but what you actually love is reading about or watching gay dudes make out so you can go on and on about how it's *so cute*. You're all for the cause until it means supporting girls making out or folks who don't want to make out with anyone or people who don't identify as boys or girls. You just want your cute boys kissing, and that's it."

The whole idea is ridiculous, but the others at the table are nodding, and my defenses snap up. "None of that's true," I say. "I support the cause because I love Dino."

Now that Kandis has found her voice, she keeps raising it to cut me down. "Not because we all deserve to be treated like human beings?"

Charlie, who acts a little younger than the others and seems eager to please them, even jumps in. "You wouldn't give a shit about none of us if you didn't know Dino."

"That's not what I'm saying." I don't know how I stepped in it so bad. I was telling stories and they were laughing and now I've screwed it up. Dino's gonna be so pissed. "Can we go back to the first thing I said?"

Jamal throws me a frown. "The thing where you made a broad generalization about gays and theater? Sure, let's do that."

"I've joked about that with Dino before," I say. "He thought it was funny. Why are you attacking me for it now?"

Kandis throws up her hands, and she's not the only one.

Shanika's glaring at me, and Gwen's shading her eyes like she can't decide whether she's embarrassed by or for me.

"First off," Kandis says, "trying to frame this as an attack is bullshit. Don't do that. Second, the shit you and Dino joke about in private isn't the same as the shit you say to people you don't know."

"Anyone ever call you a fag?" Jamal asks.

"Or a dyke?" Gwen adds.

"No," I say.

"Then those jokes don't belong to you," Kandis continues. "What you got with Dino is between you and him, but the rest of us don't want to hear that shit from some girl who thinks she's with us because she's got a gay cousin and watches RuPaul and knows how to snap."

My gut reaction is to storm off. These people don't know me. They don't know who I am or what I've suffered. They don't know what I've been through with Dino. How I supported him and ensured that no one at school talked shit about or bullied him.

Jamal catches my attention. His eyes have softened a little. "Ask yourself this too: Was Dino really laughing with you? Or was he laughing 'cause he didn't know how to tell you it wasn't funny?"

The question might as well be a knife to the gut. Dino hates conflict. He's the kind of person who'd eat food he was allergic to at someone else's house to avoid insulting them. I assumed he trusted me enough to tell me when I crossed a line, but maybe he didn't. Maybe he never had.

Gwen and Adonis drift into the house, and Charlie and Andy and Shanika move their party to the hot tub, leaving me with Jamal and Dafne and Kandis. I have a lot of thoughts about what they told me, but I don't feel confident discussing them. At least not now.

"What do y'all know about July Cooper?" I ask.

"She died," Jamal says. "Some brain shit."

Kandis smacks his arm. "She knows that. She's here for the funeral."

The dog keeps sniffing at me, so I finally pick him up. "I'm here for the wedding. Delilah's?"

Jamal gives Kandis a look. "See?"

"He didn't talk about her much," Dafne says.

"With me either," I say. "Did he mention why they stopped being friends?" Bringing this up might not be a great idea seeing as they could tell me things I won't be able to unhear, but this is my chance to find out what Dino honestly thinks of me.

Kandis slides down in her chair a little and props her feet up on a side table. "I don't know what that girl did, but it must've been pretty bad."

"Why do you say that?"

"You ever met your cousin?" she asks. "He don't get mad at nothing."

I roll my eyes thoughtlessly. "Well, that's not true," I say. "He's not a saint."

"Nah," Jamal says. "I don't think he was pissed at her."

"Why?"

"He never said a harsh word about her," Jamal says. "Only thing he ever said was how she was fun and we would've liked her."

This time Kandis rolls her eyes. "No one's more fun than me. I doubt I would've liked her."

"That's because you're a hateful troll who'd set the world on fire and watch it burn before you admitted liking anything or anyone," Dafne says, but there's a playful smile in her eyes.

Kandis nods. "True."

"It sucks she died, though," Jamal says, going on like the girls hadn't interrupted. "Sudden like that?" He shakes his head. "I had a brother die quick that way, and I never stop thinking about the shit I didn't tell him. Wondering if I could've saved him."

Kandis and Dafne glance at each other and then at him, and I want to ask more, but I get the feeling this isn't a subject Jamal needs me to drag out.

"What would you do if you died and then came back?" I ask.

"Like a zombie?" I turn around; it's Adonis with Gwen.

"Not a zombie," I say. "But everyone still thinks you're dead, so you can't see the people you love."

Dafne grimaces. "Sounds horrible."

"Yeah," Kandis says. "If I'm not dismembering my enemies and eating their brains, what's the point?"

I'm about to answer, even though I'm pretty sure it was a rhetorical question, when I feel a sharp pain where my stomach should be, followed by horrific noise that sounds like the lowest note of a trombone. Coming from me. Coming *out* of me.

The dog yelps and leaps from my lap, skittering across the deck. Everyone stops at once. Their heads swivel and turn toward me, and then Jamal raises his hand to his nose and says, "Holy shit, girl!"

I stand so fast and hard that I knock over my chair, and I run inside and lock myself in the bathroom.

DINO

LEON SPENDS THE WALK TO RAFI'S HOUSE RANTING about Gwen and Adonis. I'm grateful to him for acting like a buffer between me and Rafi and keeping us from having to discuss what he said.

Rafi loves me.

Rafi *loves* me.

Rafi loves *me*.

The last one is the most difficult to parse. In a way, I expected him to say it sooner because Rafi's full of love and he gives it away so easily. The kids at the community center are a perfect example. He's their age, but he acts like he's their big brother. They come from wherever they've been, dragging their problems behind them, and he offers them friendship and love and doesn't ask for anything in return. And they love him back whether he asks them to or not. Most of the time they don't even deserve him. But Rafi's declaration is still a surprise, and I'm not sure how I feel about it.

"I mean, who does she think she is?" Leon says for at least the tenth time. Leon's squat but muscular, and he walks like he's on his way to kill someone. The first time I met him, I thought he didn't like me, but Rafi told me he always looks that way. Resting Serial Killer Face, they call it at the center. "She's got nothing I don't have."

"You know it's not about you, right?" Rafi says.

"How are you gonna say Adonis dumped me, hooked up with Gwen, and then she brought him here to rub it in my face, but it's not about me?"

Rafi shrugs. "When you love someone and they don't love you in return, it can feel like everything they do is an attack. But most of the time, they're as confused as you are."

"So I'm just supposed to let this happen?"

"Pretty much," Rafi says.

Leon kicks a rock as we finally turn onto Rafi's street. "That's shit advice, Raf."

"Yeah, well, we don't get to control how other people feel," he says. "The only thing we get to control is how we feel. So you can keep on hurting and letting that hurt turn into hate until you get to the point where you can't even be in the same room with Adonis, or you can take the feelings you had for him and find some way to nurture them into friendship."

"Why the hell would I want that?"

Rafi glances at me before answering Leon. "Friendship with someone you love isn't a consolation prize."

I'm a little anxious when we get to the house. I hope July hasn't done anything stupid, but it's July, so I have no idea what I'm going to find.

Jamal's in my face the second we walk through the door. "Dude, your cousin locked herself in the toilet and won't come out."

Yeah, I did not see that coming.

Rafi follows me upstairs. Dafne and Kandis are standing outside the door.

"It wasn't that bad," Kandis is saying. "I've done worse; trust me."

I clear my throat. "Hey."

"Good, you're here," Dafne says. But Kandis goes, "We got this," and I'm not sure what to do.

Rafi, thankfully, does. "Hey, why don't we give Dino a minute alone with his cousin?" When no one moves, he says, "Or you can go home?" Dafne takes off, but Kandis scowls at me before heading downstairs.

"You good?" Rafi asks. I nod.

As soon as they're gone, I rap my knuckles on the door. "It's me. Dino. Open up."

A few seconds later, the door cracks open. July's eye peers out to make certain I'm alone before fully opening the door. I'm about to ask what's going on when she grabs my arm, yanks me into the bathroom, and slams the door shut again.

"What did you do?" I ask, though I'm half-joking.

Rafi's bathroom is nearly the size of his bedroom, but it's got the original hardware from the 1920s and it's always kind of reminded me of a grandma's bathroom. Not either of *my* grandmas—they have better taste than this—but somewhere out in the wide world is a grandma with questionable taste and a bathroom exactly like this one.

July sits on the edge of the tub and buries her face in her hands. I expect her to immediately lay into me for assuming she screwed up, even though I wasn't entirely serious. I sit beside her and wrap my arm around her.

"You must've done something right if you won over Kandis. She was looking feistier than a Balrog."

"Nerd," July says through her hands.

"Rafi told me he loves me." I don't actually want to talk about it—the words haven't settled into me and I haven't decided how I feel about them—but at this point, I'd sing July's favorite song while juggling knives to get her talking. "Specifically, he said he loves me and that I deserve to be loved. Which, thanks for telling me something I already know. Obviously I deserve to be loved. Right? Everyone does."

"Even serial killers?" July mumbles.

"Maybe not once they've started killing people. But definitely before that."

"What about people who drive slow in the fast lane and don't use their blinkers?"

"Of course—" I stop. "Nope. Changed my mind. Those people can die lonely and alone."

July laughs a little. Not much, but I'll take it. "What'd you say?" she asks. "When Rafi told you he loves you?"

"Cool?"

"For real? The guy opens his heart to you and you respond with 'cool'?"

"He caught me by surprise! What else was I supposed to say?"

"Do you love him?"

I shrug. "I don't know. I know that I don't not love him, but I refuse to be the kind of person who says it back when he doesn't mean it. Rafi deserves it to be real. He deserves better."

"Better than what?"

"Better than me."

July peeks between her fingers at me. "No argument here. Seriously, where'd you find that guy? He dances ballet? He writes better than me? He volunteers?"

"How did you—? Did you snoop in his room?"

"It was Roxy!" She sits up completely now. "Did you expect me not to?"

"Yes!"

"I'm beginning to doubt how well you actually know me."

"Knowing the worst about you doesn't mean I can't hope for the best." I can't rewind time and keep July from violating Rafi's privacy, so I sigh and let it go.

July wrinkles her nose and raises her eyebrows, making a face that basically says she doesn't care either way. "You should talk to him."

"And tell him what?"

"The truth is a good place to start."

"Except I don't know what the truth is."

"Yes you do," July says. "You're just afraid to say it. Like always."

I purse my lips. "What's that supposed to mean?"

"Tell your parents you hate the idea of becoming a mortician yet?"

"No, but—"

July throws on a self-satisfied smirk. "Exactly. And you never will because you're incapable of dealing with shit. All you have to do is be honest with Rafi."

I didn't want to discuss him in the first place and only brought him up to get July to talk, and since I've accomplished my goal, I decide to change the subject. "So, are you going to tell me what happened, or are we going to hide in the bathroom for the rest of the night?"

July tenses. Her back and shoulders go rigid and I worry that I pushed too soon.

"I farted."

I scoot to the side a little.

July slaps my arm. "Not now!"

"Oh."

The tension leaves her body, and she deflates. "Outside," she says. "I was talking to everyone—I might have told them about the time you were playing Robin Hood and you fell off the stage during the rescue scene and gave yourself a concussion—"

"Really?"

She ignores me. "And then this blast of gas tore out of me. It was so loud."

"Was it more like a high-pitched squeak? You know, the kind

that sneaks out and goes on forever? Or did it come out in blasts like the rat-tat-tat of a machine gun?"

July's mouth goes tight, and she stares at me like she's seriously considering the many painful ways she can murder me. But she says, "Like a sad, never-ending trumpet," and I bust up laughing.

"You always did like to toot your own horn."

And then July loses it too, and we're laughing together, really laughing. Tears are running down my eyes and my face is hot, and July would look the same way if she had tears or a working circulatory system.

"That was a terrible joke, Dino." She manages to get control of herself. "The smell was the worst, though. It was like—"

"You're literally rotting from the inside out?" I finish, holding the stitch in my side from laughing.

July nods. "I'm dead, aren't I?"

"You're not dead."

"You were right, though; I'm not alive, either. This is a real thing that's happening." She holds up her thumb. "This wasn't some fluke, was it? More of my skin might come off. And I couldn't have farted seeing as I don't have a stomach. That was decomposition gasses forcing their way out of me."

Finally, I see the full realization of her situation reflected in her eyes, and I wish I didn't. July didn't deserve to die, but she doesn't deserve this either. "Come on," I say. "We'll figure out what's happening to you. I promise."

"Everyone heard it," July says. "Everyone *smelled* it. I've never been so embarrassed in my life, and the only way you're getting me out of this bathroom is through the window."

Seeing as the only window is over the tub and about six-inches square, I doubt that plan's workable. "Sixth grade," I say.

"You'll have to be more specific. A lot of shit went down in sixth grade, most of which I've tried to forget."

"Pumpkin Pie July?"

July's hand flies to her mouth and her eyes shoot wide open. "You swore you'd never mention that."

"I'm not," I say. "But that was way worse than this, and you survived it."

"Barely."

"So what if you farted in front of them?"

"It was the unholiest of smells, Dino."

I shrug. "I held Kandis's hair on New Year's Eve while she sat in the bushes and puked ramen for an hour and tried to convince me that watching movies with Nicholas Cage in them contributes to swimming pool drowning deaths."

"Obviously," July mutters.

"Besides, they don't know you. To them, you're my random cousin whom they'll never see again."

"What if this doesn't end?"

"The gas?"

She motions at herself. "Me. Being not-dead."

"Oh. I don't know." She deserves a better answer, but the

only thing I've learned for certain since July sat up on the gurney earlier tonight is that she is definitely still decomposing. So if this *is* a miracle, it's a pretty crappy one.

July stands and walks to the sink and looks at herself in the mirror. I wish I knew what she saw in her reflection. Mirrors are liars. They never show us what's truly there. They show us what we expect to see. I have no idea what July or Rafi see when they look at me, but when I look into a mirror, I see a boy who's not quite enough. Not quite tall enough, not quite muscular enough, not quite tan enough, not quite good-looking enough. And I wonder, now, what July sees reflected.

"You wanted to figure this shit out," she says. "And I should've listened to you."

"It's not important—"

"Yeah, I think it is."

"Why?"

July stares into the mirror for another second, and then turns around. "I can't stay like this. We have to find a way to end it."

"Or fix it?"

"I don't think we can fix it. I think all we can do is end it."

JULY

IT'S NOT DINO'S TRIP DOWN EMBARRASSMENT LANE that gets me out of the bathroom. It's looking at my reflection and seeing nothing. Not the July who used to stand in front of the mirror every day and tell herself she looked damn good. Not a beautiful corpse. Just nothing. And Dino was right. These people don't know me. When they tell this story to their other friends, it won't be about the time Dino's dead best friend, July Cooper, dealt the foulest smelling gas ever dealt; they'll tell the story of how Dino's cousin, Roxy, farted. For them, Roxy is more real than July ever was.

I've been kidding myself thinking it matters how long this lasts. I'm rotting. The way I am at this moment is as good as it's going to get, and it's already not great. I stink, I'm falling apart, and my organs are in a bag in my stomach. There's no way I can inflict the pain on my parents seeing me would cause. I can't slip into to my old life, and no matter where I try to start a new one I'll still be a freak. A thing to be stared at and laughed at and pitied.

This is no life, and I need to figure out what it is and end it.

Everyone's in the living room when we come downstairs. Jamal starts clapping when he sees me, and everyone else joins in. Rafi tries to tell them to stop, but whatever. I take a bow and continue down the stairs.

"Thanks for coming to the show," I say. "Good night!" And then I head toward the door.

Dino motions for Rafi to walk us out.

"You really have to go?" he says when we're standing outside. "If it's the gas problem, I have pills you can take."

I shake my head at the same time as Dino says, "Funeral tomorrow."

Rafi nods solemnly. He holds Dino's hand. "It was nice meeting you, Roxy. Sorry we didn't get to spend more time together."

"Yeah. It was good to finally meet you."

Dino coughs and says, "Do you mind waiting in the car? I want to talk to Rafi."

I catch the look he's giving me and smile. "Take however long you need." Then I turn to Rafi before I leave. "Hey, Rafi, I'm sorry."

"For?"

"Some dumb thing I said that I shouldn't have. Just, I'm sorry." I leave them standing there, both looking a little confused.

I wish I could eavesdrop on Dino and Rafi's conversation, but I can barely even make out their expressions in the shadows. I'm surprised there's not more kissing. Or any kissing, actually.

It looks like Dino's doing most of the talking, which is unusual. Eventually I get bored and turn my focus to my own problem. I know I died, but not much else. Everything from my last dinner until I woke up at DeLuca and Son's is blank. There's nothing there. Which is a terrifying thought in itself that I have to gloss over so I don't spiral off into an existential crisis. I don't know what's animating me or how long I can expect this to last. I do know that my body is continuing to decompose. According to Dino, other people who should be dead aren't, and that seems like a place to begin.

I think I've come up with a half-baked, not-great-but-good-enough plan by the time Dino gets into the car. His mouth is turned down and he doesn't look as happy as I expected he'd be. Before I can ask how it went with Rafi, he says, "What was that about?"

"I'm gonna need a little more than that."

"The apology?"

"Oh, that," I say. "Jokes aren't funny if everyone's not in on them."

"That's it?"

I don't understand why Dino sounds upset. "I said something I shouldn't have, and I needed to say I was sorry. Better late than never. Are you pissed?"

"No." Dino starts the car and takes off, though I don't know to where. I can tell by the set of his jaw and the way he won't look at me that, despite what he said, he's definitely upset.

"What?"

"You never say you're sorry to me, but you meet Rafi for five whole seconds and you're throwing out apologies like confetti!"

"You're mad that I apologized to your boyfriend but not to you?"

"He's not my boyfriend anymore."

"Stop the car!"

Dino slams on the brakes, and thank God we're in a residential neighborhood or someone might have rear ended us.

"Metaphorically, asshole!" I shout.

"Don't yell at me while I'm driving! Are you trying to kill us?" Dino pounds his fist on the steering wheel.

There are so many things I want to say, most of them involve telling him where he can stick sharp, spiky objects, but I calm myself before speaking. "Why isn't Rafi your boyfriend? Did he break up with you?"

"No."

"You broke up with him?"

"Yes."

"Why would you do something so stupid?"

Dino rounds on me. "You told me to be honest!"

"I didn't mean for you to dump him."

"I'm done talking about this."

My brain is trying to figure out how Dino got from "be honest" to "dump your perfect boyfriend." I'd meant for him to explain to Rafi that he didn't know if he loved him and needed time to figure it out, which I'm pretty certain Rafi would have happily given him, but if Dino won't talk about it, I can't force him.

"Are you seriously pissed off that I apologized to him and not to you?"

"Can we not talk about anything remotely connected to Rafi? Great. Thanks."

Dino's shut down. It's virtually impossible to get through to him when he's like this. If we were still best friends and I wasn't a rotting corpse, I'd suggest we drown our feelings in chocolate and violent video games, but I know that can't happen.

"I doubt you're up for it," I say, "but how would you feel about a trip to the hospital?"

Dino lets out an exhausted sigh. "Why?"

"Because I have an idea. It's just probably not a good one."

DINO

"HELP?" I DRAG JULY THROUGH THE AUTOMATIC SLIDING doors, regretting agreeing to this plan. July is dead weight, and I don't lift much that's heavier than a sandwich, but also this idea is ludicrous and bound to fail. At the same time, my ex–best friend returned from the dead and I broke up with a guy who's basically perfect, so lots of things that shouldn't be happening are.

The emergency room chairs are filled with people, most of whom look exhausted and worried. Straight across from the doors is a glass window. A nurse behind the desk pops up and disappears, and ten seconds later rushes out to meet us.

"What's wrong?"

"She's dead."

"Dead?" the nurse asks. "Are you sure?"

"Does she look alive to you?" I raise my voice a little to make my point, and two minutes later, July's on a bed in the hallway.

The nurse tells us they're short staffed and busy and that some-one will help when they're available, but based on the skeptical and exhausted tone in her voice, I'm not expecting that we'll be seen soon. Which is a good thing.

July sits up. "See?"

"That's creepy," I say.

"What?"

"That you can lie perfectly still like that." I grimace. "For a second, I thought you were actually dead again."

"I wish," July says. "Now what?"

I whip my head around to face July. "This was *your* plan."

July wears a satisfied grin. "And it worked. I got us inside the hospital. Now it's your turn. Do some science and figure out why I'm not-dead."

"This is a hospital, not a lab." I stare at her incredulously. "What do you expect me to do? Take your temperature? Your blood pressure?"

"Sounds like a decent place to start?"

"I already know the results! No heart, no blood pressure."

July's enthusiasm seems to be waning. A moment later, she slips off the edge of the bed and heads toward one of the rooms.

"Where are you going?"

"If you can't help me, maybe there's someone else here who can." She peeks into the first room, moves onto the next, peeks in it, and then slips inside, leaving me to stand by her now-empty bed wondering how I got mixed up in this. July was right, though. For most of the night I'd been complaining that we needed to figure out what was happening, but the truth is that this is far beyond my abilities. Even with access to a laboratory filled with fancy equipment, I wouldn't know where to begin. Should I look for physiological evidence or for answers in the realm of the divine?

I get why July thought it would be a good idea to sneak into a hospital, but solving the mystery of July Cooper is going to require help from someone much smarter than me.

"Dino." July pokes her head out of the room. "You've got to see this."

The room is crowded with three beds separated by curtains. July leads me behind one curtain where a woman is lying in a bed with leads stuck to her chest, and wires running in a bundle to machines that silently mark her heartbeat. She's about my mom's age. Dark hair, puffy skin, the right side of her head and face are covered with gauze, but something's wrong. It's like that half of her face is collapsed.

"What—"

"A chunk of her head is gone, Dino."

"That can't be," I say. But I move closer to her and measure the geometry of her face. The woman's eye follows me as my brain comes to the only conclusion it can. "She should be dead."

"Ma'am? Can you hear me?" July snaps her fingers in front of the woman's good eye but doesn't get a response.

"She won't answer," says a voice from one of the other beds. It's followed by violent retching. "Accidental shooting. More brain missing than is left."

"This is my fault," July whispers.

I start to tell her it's not, that it can't be, but I'm interrupted by vomiting, which July leaves to investigate. Maybe this is July's fault. Not intentionally. She's a lot of things, but she'd never willfully cause this kind of suffering to another person.

"I'm so sorry," I say to the woman. I don't know if she can hear or understand me, but I hope she's not in pain.

I follow July to the next bed. It's occupied by a guy holding a pan on his chest filled with black sludge that looks like tar. His body shudders and he sits forward and pukes into the pan. More of the black stuff pours out of his mouth. Tears stream down his eyes and he wipes them and then his mouth with his hand.

"What happened to you?" July says.

"Took too many pills." His voice is raw.

"On purpose?"

I smack July's arm. "You can't ask someone that."

But the guy nods. He looks like he's maybe in his twenties, though it's difficult to tell. His hair is receding and he looks exhausted and threadbare.

"Did you die?" This time when I try to interrupt July, she slaps me away.

The man shakes his head. "Should've," the man says. "Doctor said so. We should all be dead."

"We?" I ask.

The guy motions weakly at the bed with the woman in it. "Her, everyone. Overheard a nurse say no one's dying that ought to."

Until now we'd only had the word of the paramedic at

Monty's that people had stopped dying, but this guy and the woman missing half her brain prove it's true. July isn't the only anomaly.

"Why?" July asks.

We have to wait for the guy to throw up again before he can answer. I can't believe how much of that black stuff is coming up. Now that I know why he's here, I guess that it's charcoal. When he finishes, he says, "You know what depression feels like?"

This isn't the "why" July wanted to know about. She meant to ask why he wasn't dead. I expect her to interrupt and rephrase the question. Instead she says, "No. Why don't you explain it."

"Imagine you're in a room with everyone you care about. Partying. Enjoying yourself. They're laughing and having fun. You are too." He coughs and spits out more charcoal. "Then it changes. Gets dark. You can still see your friends, but they can't see you. Can't hear you. You can't touch them or get them to pay attention to you."

"That sounds like a nightmare," I say, though I don't mean to say it out loud.

The man nods. "And there's a voice whispering that you deserve to be alone. That they never liked you and only pretended to be your friend out of pity. That they're so much happier when you're not with them. You don't want to believe the voice, but you know deep in your heart that the voice speaks only the truth."

July inches nearer to the bed. "So you decided to take some pills and end it?"

"Why bother with life if it's nothing but pain?"

"That's ridiculous," July says. "You wouldn't cut off your hand if you got a splinter in your finger."

"You might if it got infected and gangrenous."

"We should go, July," I say. Arguing with someone who attempted to take their own life isn't a good idea, and I don't see how it helps us figure out why July's not-dead, but July ignores me.

"How do you feel now?" she asks. "You didn't die. The doctor told you that you should have died, but you didn't. They put that charcoal shit in you and it'll get the poison out, and you're going to live." July looks at the man expectantly. "You're glad for the second chance, right?"

The man shakes his head. "If the next words out of your mouth have to do with Jesus, I'm dumping this pan over your head."

I hear voices outside of the room heading our way.

"Then what's the point?" July says.

"Exactly."

We can't risk being caught in this room, so I pull July toward the door and peer out. Two nurses are walking in our direction. I do the only thing I can think of, and grab July and run. One of the nurses sees us and yells, but I don't have time to see if we're being followed.

A doctor in a white coat makes a grab for me but only gets a handful of my sleeve, which I twist out of his grasp.

"Come on!" I burst into a stairwell and run up. July and I climb to the top and out onto the roof. I gently shut the door and lead July behind a huge AC unit. It's big enough to hide us from being seen, but so loud that we won't be able to hear anyone if they sneak up on us.

I'm sweaty and gross, but we're so close to the intracoastal that there's a light breeze coming off the water, and it feels amazing. The moon is three-quarters waxing and hangs overhead, seeming to loom much larger than normal.

I give July a couple of minutes to collect herself, hoping she'll decide to talk on her own, but she sits on the gravel roof with her knees pulled to her chest, rocking from side to side.

"You said you wanted to figure out why you were not-dead, not to interrogate someone who tried to end their life."

"That woman," July says. "You think she was in pain?"

"I hope not."

"What do you think happens to her if this thing ends?"

Neither of us even knows what this "thing" is, so guessing when or how it ends is useless, but I say, "I hope she'll be allowed to die."

"And the other guy?" July says. "Do you think he'll die too?"

"I don't know."

July looks at me. "Neither do I. This should be a good thing. People get hurt, like the guy who got hit by the car outside Monty's, but they don't die, which gives their bodies a chance to heal."

God, Monty's feels like forever ago, but it was only a couple of hours. "I don't think there's any way to fix what's wrong with the woman we saw."

"Why is this happening if it's not to make people better?" she says. "I want to go home, but I can't. It'd be cruel to make my parents live with my decomposing corpse or to spend a few days or weeks with me and then have to lose me for a second time. No matter what, I'd be hurting them.

"I thought I could live with this if it helped other folks, but what the hell good is it if it means they're going to suffer like that woman or if they don't want to live in the first place?"

July stops and cocks her head to the side.

I get on my belly and slowly poke my head around the condenser. Two doctors are standing by the door smoking. They both look haggard, but I can't hear what they're saying. I've never understood how doctors can smoke. It's like a firefighter deliberately disabling the smoke detectors in her house and then setting fire to her couch.

We wait for them to finish, and I consider what July was saying. It seems like a miracle on the surface—no one dies; everyone lives—but based on what we've witnessed, the miracle looks more like torture. And I get why July might think it hopeless, but we've only seen a small piece of what's going on. She doesn't have the whole picture.

Eventually, the doctors finish their break and leave.

"Go on," I tell her.

But the fire's burned out of July. She's sunken in on herself. "That guy didn't want to live—he still doesn't. Who are we to deny him what he wants?"

"That's silly and you know it," I say. "Depression isn't rational.

I read once that the majority of people who survived jumping off the Golden Gate Bridge said they regretted jumping immediately after doing it."

"Did that guy look filled with regret?"

"No," I say, "But here he'll get help. This time he's been given could be exactly what he needs to realize he made a mistake and that life *is* worth living."

She throws up her hands. "Good for him, but what about the woman missing part of her brain? What about me?"

"Look, I know you don't want to see your parents or Jo because you think it'll hurt them too much to see you like this, but I think you're wrong. I think they'd gladly take that pain for the chance to see you, even if you are gassy and falling apart."

"Stop," she says in a low voice.

"I'm not saying you could take up your old life or even that your life would resemble normal, but you could at least be with the people who love you most in the world. You don't have to do this alone."

"Stop," she says, a little louder.

"And I know we're not friends and that this one night didn't erase the things we did to each other over the last year, but I'll look after you. I'll keep more of your skin from sliding off, and I'll keep government scientists from taking you away to perform gruesome experiments on you. Friends or not, I've got your back."

"Stop it, Dino! Just fucking stop!" This time July yells. She takes my hand and looks into my eyes, and I know what she's going to say before she says it. "I died. And unlike these other folks, I was meant to die and to stay dead. I don't know what cosmic mistake caused this, but it's time to correct it."

JULY

DINO DOESN'T TALK ON THE DRIVE TO HIS HOUSE, AND
I'm not in the mood to chat either, so I let the silence ride in the
backseat. I think Dino was right that I should have never left
DeLuca and Son's when I woke up. It was stupid to think I could
rise from the dead and pretend life was shiny and grand, but
that's over now. It's time for July Cooper to face reality.

"You think your parents are still awake?" I ask when we roll
up to his house.

Dino shakes his head. "Dad's in bed by eleven every night,
and Mom doesn't go out dancing as often as she used to."

"Oh."

Dino kills the lights and the engine, and we sit in the car. I
think he's waiting for me to get out, but I'm not quite ready.

"Tell me the truth. Why did you break up with Rafi?"

"I said—"

"Spill it, Dino." I said I was ready to face reality, but I didn't mean this exact second.

Dino grips the steering wheel. "It's not complicated," he says. "He told me he loved me and that I deserve to be loved."

"You already went over this part."

"Well, so does he."

"You don't love him?"

Dino's fidgety. He won't stop moving. Tapping his fingers, squeezing the wheel, jiggling his knees. He's going to rattle into pieces. "I'm seventeen, and we've only been together a year. How the hell am supposed to know? Either way, he should be with someone who *does* know."

"Did he say that?"

"No, but—"

"So you made the decision for him?" I shake my head. This boy is never going to survive without me. "Rafi's pretty close to perfect. And his friends are okay too."

Dino glances my direction. "I thought you'd be happier about this. Doing a little dance, singing a jaunty song."

"Right," I say. "Because all I've ever wanted was for your relationship to fail and you to be miserable." I throw my hands in the air. "You found me out. I'm a monster."

"There's something wrong with me," Dino says.

"I've been saying that since the day we met."

He ignores me. "I didn't plan on breaking up with him. I thought about what you said, how I should be honest with him, and that's what I was planning. I was going to tell him that I didn't know if I loved him, but that if he was willing to give me time to figure it out, I'd like that."

"Clearly those aren't the words you said."

Dino purses his lips. "I started thinking how it was unfair to make him wait for me to discover who I am and what I want. And how, if I couldn't make *our* friendship work, what chance did I have with Rafi?"

"That's ridiculous," I say. "Our friendship is nothing like your relationship."

"Isn't it? You were my best friend, and I screwed it up. No matter how I feel about Rafi now or in the future, the chances of me ruining everything are practically 100 percent." He hangs his head. "Guess I haven't changed as much as you thought, have I?"

Like always, a clever retort pops up immediately, but this time I push it down and take a second to consider what I want to say. "You act like you don't care, like you aren't proud of dressing up for Rafi and aren't happy to help him talk one of his friends off a ledge, but it's not true. You do care; you *are* proud. Rafi and his friends bring out a better side of you."

"Better than what?"

"Better than what I bring out."

"That's not true."

I said it out of instinct, but the more I think about it, the truer it feels. "Look at us. Instead of appreciating the miracle of my resurrection or going on a grand adventure to track down the truth of my return, I caused a car accident; I stole your car, was recognized, and nearly got you arrested; I lied to and farted decomposition gasses on your friends; I gave you advice that you somehow interpreted to mean you should break up with your boyfriend; and we've been fighting nonstop."

Dino growls. "The accident wasn't your fault, and you didn't fart *on* my friends. Just near them."

"Bad enough."

"Come on, July. You're the one who helped me see that working in the mortuary wasn't the future I wanted."

"Some help," I say. "You had a life planned out, and I trashed it and left you with nothing to take its place."

Dino sighs. "Figuring out my life isn't your job."

"It should be," I say. "You're pretty terrible at it."

"Me?" he says. "It's not like your life was on a fast track to success before you . . ."

"Died?"

"Yeah."

"At least I was happy," I say. "At least I was doing what I enjoyed instead of moping and shitting on other people for being happy."

"What're you even talking about?"

I turn toward Dino and give him my best "you know what I'm talking about" face. It's a good one. I spent hours perfecting it in the mirror. "Good luck?"

"That's what you're mad about?"

"Among other things," I say. "It was opening night. You could've walked by me without saying a word like you'd done a hundred other times in the halls at school, but you looked me dead in the eye and said 'Good luck.' Were you trying to kill me?"

Dino bows his head. "I only came backstage to say hi to Benji and Dan. I didn't expect you to come strolling out of the boys' dressing room. You surprised me, and I said the first thing that came to mind."

I frown and nod knowingly. "It says a lot that your instinct was to curse me."

"It's not a curse!" he yells. "It's a ridiculous superstition!"

"Ridiculous to you," I say. "Saying that to me the way you did? You may as well have shoved me off the stage and stood over my bloody body, cackling."

Now Dino rolls his eyes and, okay, maybe I went a little too far with that last one. "Did you get hurt?" he asks. "No. You were fine. The performance was fine."

"Actually, I got a tickle in my throat and couldn't hit the high note during my solo, ruining the whole number."

"If I didn't notice, trust me, no one else did either."

"So if it's not important to you, then it doesn't matter?"

"Says the girl who abandoned me at Walmart to go to 7-Eleven, nearly got arrested, and gaslighted a schoolmate to save her own ass."

Enough. I get out of the car and slam the door and stomp to the rear entrance of the funeral home. My plan was to also walk in there and slam *that* door behind me in the most dramatic fashion possible, but the door's locked, so I have to stand in the shadows and wait for Dino to decide to get his ass out of the car and let me in.

When he does, I shove him aside and march to where this nightmare began.

"Why are we here?" Dino asks. "What's the plan?" There's an edge to his voice, but mostly he sounds weary, and I understand the feeling.

"I'm through." I motion at my rotting body. "I need this to end."

"But how?" Dino asks. "We wasted the whole night, and we still don't know why or how you're even possible."

"Look, rising from the dead was like waking up." I shrug, trying to look casual, like none of this is touching me. I hope Dino's buying it. "So maybe dying is as simple as going back to sleep."

"Do you honestly believe that?"

"Yes." We square off and stare at one another for a moment. "Why do you care? Didn't you say there needed to be a funeral tomorrow? Well here I am."

Dino keeps standing there with his arms hanging limp like he can't believe this is his life. "I only said that to convince you to tell someone about our situation."

"That's not happening."

"What if this doesn't work?" Dino asks. "What if you try to go to sleep and you can't? Are you going to let them bury you alive?"

"I'm not alive."

"Whatever!"

I cross to Dino and rest my hands on his shoulders. "I can't go on like this. Let me try it my way. You can check on me tomorrow. If I'm still not-dead, we'll tell my parents. Okay?"

Dino clenches his jaw, and I can practically hear him grinding his teeth trying to come up with an objection. "Why do you think this will work? Just tell me that."

"I'm July Cooper," I say. "Have you ever known me to not get what I want?"

"No, but—"

"Then, let's do this." I move toward the gurney and hop up.

"Wait," Dino says.

"Look, whatever sappy bullshit you're going to say, save it for my funeral. Bury our past with me and let it stay buried."

Dino shakes his head. "I was going to ask you to get undressed first."

"Oh. Fine. Definitely don't want you doing it for me."

"Trust me. There's nothing I want to see less than your naked body." Dino tosses me the sheet I'd woken up covered in and then turns around without being asked.

I shimmy out of my clothes, folding each piece and setting it aside. "Why, because girls are icky?"

"No, because I kind of loathe you. Also, you're like a sister, and no one wants to see their sister naked."

I finish getting undressed. My brain understands that the temperature is lower, and part of me recognizes that I should be cold and shivering, but there's a disconnect between my brain and body. It wasn't this noticeable when I first woke up; the longer I'm not-dead, the less I feel.

I climb onto the gurney and lie down. "Done."

Dino turns back around. I expect him to wheel me into the freezer so he can be done with me, but he goes to one of the cabinets and gets some supplies.

"What're you doing?"

"I have to fix your thumb so my parents don't notice that your skin tore off."

"Oh." I lie there thinking about what I'm doing while Dino smears what looks like spackle around the edges of the tear. This is the best option. I died. Fate or God or the natural order of the universe decided it was time for me to die. If I was meant to live, Dr. Larsen would have found the weak blood vessel in my brain when Momma took me to see her for my migraines and she did a million different scans and tests. This, what's happening to me, isn't natural. If there's one lesson I've learned tonight, it's that no good comes of trying to bring back what's dead.

"That should be good enough."

I hold up my thumb. I wouldn't know my skin had slipped off if it hadn't been my skin that had slipped off. "You really are kind of talented at this."

"So everyone keeps saying." Dino motions at it. "Try not to move your thumb. Like, at all." He stands by the freezer. "You certain about this?"

I stretch out my arms and fake a yawn. "If it means not having to see your face again, then I'm definitely ready."

Dino opens the door and the first thing I see is another body covered by a sheet.

"Hell no," I say. "I ordered a single room. No way I'm sharing freezer space with some other corpse."

"Mr. Alire," Dino says.

"I don't give a shit who it is."

"The lights will go off when I close the door," Dino says, "so you won't even see him."

"You think that makes it better?"

Dino lets the door shut. The lock clicks into place. "I can leave you out here, and you can wheel yourself into the freezer when you're ready."

As if I'm ever going to be ready to sleep next to some dead old dude. But I nod anyway. "Yeah. Fine."

"Okay," Dino says. "So, I guess this is good-bye."

"Later."

"If this doesn't work—"

"We'll tell someone. Your parents or mine."

"Promise?"

"Oh my God, will you leave already?"

Dino holds up his hands and heads for the door.

Now that he's actually leaving, I'm not so sure I want him to. Every doubt I have rushes in to fill the space he's vacating. I don't know if this ridiculous plan of mine—which, if I'm being honest, isn't much of a plan—will work, and if it does, then I'll die alone, and no one should have to die alone. But if he doesn't go, I'm afraid this won't work. There are so many things I want to say to him, but the only word I manage to spit out is, "Slurpees."

Dino stops and turns around. "What?"

"That's what I went to 7-Eleven for. Slurpees."

He pauses. "Yeah. That machine's always broken. You should've gone to the one off Central." He leaves and shuts the door behind him.

DINO

FUNERALS AREN'T FOR THE DEAD. DESPITE JULY'S protestations, the dead don't actually care what outfit they're buried in. They don't care what kind of coffin they're resting in when they're lowered into the ground. The dead don't care about the font or size of the lettering on their headstones, or even what their headstones say. Those are concerns for the living. For the people left behind. Funerals are our last opportunity to show the world how much we cared about the person who died.

Over the years I've witnessed quite a few funerals, and my "favorites" were the ones where it seemed like the people left behind were competing to see who could grieve the loudest. I'm not saying that they were faking, but grief isn't loud. Grief is quiet. Grief is a strangled cry. Tears we hide. A scream in a vacuum where sound doesn't carry. And though we try to share it, grief is ultimately a burden each of us must carry alone.

I didn't cry for July when my dad told me she was dead, and I didn't cry when I left her in the prep room. I'm not heartless, but I don't know what losing July means to me yet. We were friends. Then we were enemies. She was dead, then she was not-dead. I don't know why she returned last night. Maybe some divine power hoped we'd mend the rift between us. At best we cobbled together a rickety bridge that enabled us to meet in the middle for a few hours and fight there instead of yelling at each other across a chasm.

I suspect it's going to take some time for me to figure out what July's life and death honestly mean to me, but the one thing I know for sure is that when and if I do cry for her, I'll do so quietly and alone.

"Headache?"

Delilah's sitting at the kitchen table in a bathrobe when I wander downstairs in the morning.

"Like a dog's humping my eyeballs from the back side." I stumble toward the table and stop at the chair to regain my balance.

"That's a horrifying mental image." Dee grabs me a glass of water and a couple of ibuprofen.

"Thanks."

"You should get Mom to take you to the doctor."

I shake my head and grenades detonate in my skull. "I'm fine."

"You've been getting headaches a lot lately."

"Stop worrying," I say. "Besides, it's not like seeing a doctor helped July."

Delilah purses her lips but lets it go. "You ready for the funeral?"

"No." I toss the pills into my mouth and chug the water.

"When are you scheduled to work at the diner?"

That stupid summer job I took, mostly to spite my parents, seems like something that happened to someone else a long time ago. "Not until after your wedding."

"Good," she says. "You deserve to enjoy at least a little of your summer."

"I guess." I wouldn't call any of this fun, though. "Where are Mom and Dad?"

"They already left to take the body to the church."

"Did you see her?"

I hold my breath and wait for her answer. I think I've been holding my breath since I walked away from July last night. Her plan to simply decide to be dead again seemed too simple to actually work, and I spent what was left of the night expecting her to climb through my window or sneak into my room. Dee hesitates and then nods. "You did a great job on her makeup."

I should have known better than to underestimate July. She's more stubborn than death. The strange thing is that when I finally let go of that breath, I realize I was hoping for a different answer. That there's a small part of me that wanted her to still be not-dead and for us to have more time together. I'd take an eternity fighting with her over nothing.

Delilah gives me her practiced consolatory smile. It's the same one she wears with clients that's intended to convey that she's here for you in your time of need, but isn't personally invested in your pain. "Don't worry, brother. It'll be over soon."

DINO

I STAND AT THE REAR OF THE CROWD WHILE PASTOR Johannes speaks over July's grave. The sun beams down on us from a cloudless blue sky, and the air is hot and thick. July chose a terrible time of year to die. In the confusion caused by my morning headache, I forgot to put on an undershirt, and I can feel the sweat spreading across my back and under my arms. I won't be able to take my jacket off even once I'm at July's house for the reception.

Everything's been happening in a blur. I couldn't approach July during the wake, but I saw her from afar. She looked . . . No. I'm not going to say she looked peaceful or any of that crap. She looked like a body. That's it. At some point I know I gave my condolences to Mr. and Mrs. Cooper and to Joëlle, who smiled stoically. Some of July's other friends from school were there. Benji and Neko and Sara and Kamilah. Benji tried to talk to me, but his words sounded like he was speaking an alien language, and all I could do was stare at him. They kept their distance after that. Zora Hood showed up, stayed long enough to see the body, and then ran out again. Maybe one day I'll find her and tell her the truth so she doesn't spend the rest of her life wondering if she was delusional.

The church service was long and boring, and then I helped carry the closed coffin to the hearse with a bunch of July's cousins, most of whom were polite though appropriately sedate. When we arrived at Trinity Cemetery and I took my place to unload the casket and walk it to the gravesite, I stumbled and nearly dropped July.

Mrs. Cooper, who didn't mention me stopping by last night, invited me to stand near the front with the family, but I don't deserve it. The front is a place of honor for people who loved July and for people she loved in return, and I'm not clear where either of us stand on that issue.

Sweat runs into my eyes, and I use a napkin I stuffed in my pocket on the way to the cemetery to mop my brow.

Finally. They turn the crank to lower the coffin into the ground.

My phone buzzes against my chest. I'd put it on silent but forgot to turn off vibrate too. A couple of people I don't know standing nearby glance at me and frown. I ignore it. It buzzes again. More annoyed glares. I should at least stop whoever it is from bothering me.

I pull out my phone and thumb in my lock code covertly before looking at the screen. Two messages. I have no idea who they're from. Mom and Dad and Delilah know better than to bother me, I don't expect to hear from Rafi, and, yeah, those are the only people who've texted me in the last year.

I sneak a peek at the messages and drop my phone with a gasp.

Now people are really paying attention to me, so I mouth "Sorry" and quickly crouch to retrieve my phone. I hold it close to my chest and slowly look.

Staring at me from the screen is a selfie of July flashing her best July grin. From inside her coffin.

I peel off from the group and dash around the corner. I hide behind an ostentatious mausoleum that has an iron gate and stained-glass windows so that I can look at the photos without anyone seeing. It's definitely July. In one selfie she's giving me the finger and she added a text bubble with the words, "I told you not to let them bury me in this dress!" In another she's baring her teeth and added a picture of a cartoon brain to it and the words "Nom, nom, nom." There are at least a dozen more, none of them funny, though I bet July thinks they are.

DINO: July?
DINO: Is this a joke? Is that really you?
DINO: July???

She doesn't respond. But it has to be her. I knew her stupid idea wouldn't work. She's still alive. Not-dead. Whatever. Or maybe someone's pranking me. No. No one would do that. If it's July, though, why isn't she answering? And where the hell did she get a phone?

"Dino?"

Shit! I press the lock button on my phone and step onto the path, nearly running my father down.

"You okay, son?"

My dad's wearing his funeral suit. Plain, black. Unlike my mom, it's pretty much the only outfit he owns in black.

"What're you doing here? I thought you left."

Dad nods. "Decided to stick around. Pay my respects. Saw you take off."

"I'm fine."

My father is a man of few words. Sometimes people tell me I inherited that from him, but it's not that I feel I have nothing to say, it's that what I have to say rarely feels valuable. My dad though, he watches. Waits. Speaks when he feels like it and usually feels like what he's saying has merit.

"I saw what you did with July." My breath catches in my throat for a second, but then Dad claps my shoulder. "I'm proud of you."

"God, Dad, can we not?"

"If you can put aside your feelings to prepare your best friend, then you belong in the business."

I can't do this. But I don't want to argue with him at July's funeral either, especially not with her sending me selfies from inside the casket. I grip my phone tightly, my palms sweaty, ready for it to buzz again, but it remains still and quiet.

"I should get back to the funeral."

Dad nods and sends me on my way.

JULY

OF COURSE MY *BATTERY* DIES. FUCKING FIGURES THE ONLY
thing dead in this coffin is the one thing that shouldn't be.

JULY

DINO'S GONNA LOVE RUBBING MY NOSE IN THIS ONE.
Telling me how I ended up spending most of the day and night
in a coffin because I was too pig-headed to admit I didn't have
the first clue what I was doing. But what else could I do? Let me
spin out how else things could have gone down.

Scenario 1: The kind-of-dead, rotting corpse of July Cooper
knocks on the front door of the house she once called home.
Her mother, bleary-eyed and groggy, answers the door, sees
the puffy, ashy, decaying face of her recently deceased daughter, screams, faints, and hits her head on the tile floor. July's
younger sister, Joëlle, hears the scream, rushes downstairs, and
finds zombie July hovering over the body of their comatose
mother. Jo doesn't understand what she's seeing, grabs a shovel
from the garage, smashes July's head in, and then cuts it off and
burns the body just to be sure. July's mother wakes up shortly

after. Two days later Mrs. Cooper drops dead. She'd developed a subdural hematoma from hitting her head on the tile.

Scenario 2: Dead July goes to see her father at his apartment. He's not there when she knocks—probably at work—so she lets herself in with her key and waits for him to return. Later that evening, Mr. Cooper comes home from work. Upon seeing the daughter he believed to be dead, he has a heart attack and dies.

Scenario 3: Taking the dubious advice of her once–best friend, July Cooper reveals her undeath to Dino DeLuca's parents. Mr. DeLuca is rendered unable to move other than to sit in a chair and clean his glasses, but Mrs. DeLuca has been preparing for a moment like this her entire life. As a young woman, Jenn had believed there were things beyond life that defied explanation—vampires and witches and zombies—even though she'd found no evidence of them. As she grew older, married, and had children of her own, she never stopped believing that one day she would discover the truth. And now the truth was standing in front of her in the form of her son's ex–best friend. Jenn DeLuca abandons the funeral business and reveals July's existence to the world. They become overnight superstars who go on tour so that everyone can see the girl who cheated death. But one night, as they're leaving a venue, the rowdy crowd turns violent. They want what July has. They want to live forever. They rush July and Mrs. DeLuca and tear them to pieces, carrying tiny bits home to their families, and July Cooper is forgotten by the next news cycle.

Scenario 4: Evil. Government. Scientists.

Scenario 5: The slowly decomposing but still animated corpse of July Cooper flees Palm Shores and travels the world. Being that she doesn't need to eat or breathe or sleep, she can hide anywhere—in the darkest hold of a cargo ship, in the trunk of a car, in the luggage compartment of an airplane—which she does. Over the years, she visits countries she never dreamed she'd see. She explores the world in a way only someone who's died and come back could. Yes, she continues to rot, but eventually her body attains a kind of desiccated equilibrium that, while not pretty, works for her. But while July explores the world, she's not part of it, and therefore doesn't realize that death remains suspended so long as she goes on. Prior to July Cooper's mysterious reanimation, roughly 151,000 people died throughout the world each day, which figured to 55 million per year, and 129 million babies were born, adding a total of approximately 74 million people a year to the population of an already overcrowded planet. But with death on a hiatus, population growth doubles overnight. In five years, there are over half-a-billion new mouths to feed. In ten years, overcrowding leads to food shortages, wars, global destruction, and plagues.

See? There's no scenario where I stay not-dead and things work out peachy. I had to try my stupid idea, even if it meant winding up stuck in this coffin with a dead phone, hoping Dino got my selfies and comes to dig my ass up so we can figure out how to end it for real. And, no, I don't want to think about what happens if Dino didn't get my messages or if he decides I'm too much of a hassle and that he's better off leaving me in the ground.

Thank God I'm not claustrophobic.

DINO

I WONDER HOW JULY'S HOUSE FELT TO HER WHEN SHE broke in last night. And would it be considered breaking in since she lived here? These are the questions I think about as I stand in the corner avoiding the hundred different relatives of July's who keep trying to force feed me ham salad and fried chicken and green bean casserole and some kind of jiggly Jell-O nonsense that I'm pretty certain has broccoli suspended in it.

I've met different members of July's family before. Her cousins Joel and Lucia stayed with her for a few weeks the summer between seventh and eighth grades, her aunts on her father's side visit for the holidays every couple of years. Her grandparents, of course. But I didn't realize her family was so big. I met a guy who flew in from Alaska for this, which will make July happy.

Speaking of July, I haven't heard from her since the messages at the cemetery. If I couldn't pull them up and look at them, I might be tempted to believe they were the product of a delusion brought on by grief or guilt or lack of sleep. But every time I use the bathroom, I look at the photos for the hundredth time, and they're definitely real.

So why hasn't July answered? The simplest reason is that she's dead. Aside from seeing her in the casket at the service, I don't know what happened after I left her. Sending those selfies might have been the last thing she did before she closed her eyes and died for good. Of course, there are a million other possible reasons. July's toying with me, she can't get reception, she dropped the phone and it slid down near her feet and there isn't enough room for her to reach it, her battery died, she's turned into an actual brain-eating zombie and her ravenous hunger has stolen her ability to read.

Honestly, there's only one way to know for certain, and I'm working hard to avoid thinking about it.

It's weird to see July's parents in the same house again, even though they're hanging out in different spots. Mr. Cooper is in his favorite recliner in front of the TV with some of the older men. They're talking a little too loudly, a little too animatedly. It's like they've forgotten they're at a funeral. It's not abnormal though. I've seen it hundreds of times. Husbands enduring hours of condolences with smiles plastered on their faces, brothers and boyfriends and fathers cracking jokes while everyone else barely holds it together. Men who've been taught that emotions are a weakness, and they're never to show weakness, so they bottle it up and camouflage it with laughter or anger or silence. Anything to avoid exposing that they care.

Mrs. Cooper's with a rotating group of people in the dining room. She's sitting with her elbows on the table and her chin in her hands, staring into space. Gone is the woman I saw last night. Gone is the woman offering hugs to family members at the church. Here, in her home, she doesn't feel the need to pretend. Her oldest daughter is gone, ripped out of her life, and she's struggling one second at a time to keep from screaming and screaming and screaming until she can't scream anymore.

None of these people would know what to do if Mr. or Mrs. Cooper really let out their grief. Stare while pretending not to stare and then quietly go back to shoveling potato salad into their faces, probably.

I don't notice Benji until he's standing beside me at the sliding glass windows that overlook the pool. He's got this weird evil-Muppet vibe that I thought was hot for, like, two seconds the first time I met him. Apparently he also thought I was cute when we met, but thankfully we were both too shy to say so. A relationship between us would have been an epic disaster.

"Hey, Dino. Doing okay?" Before I can answer, he rushes ahead in a torrent of words. "Stupid question. Why do people ask that? Of course you're not okay. None of us are okay. Our friend died. How is any of this going to make it okay? Being around these people, wearing this stupid suit, sharing memories of July like this'll fix anything. Mostly, I want to break stuff or set something on fire and watch it burn. Maybe the school. Torching the school might make me feel a little better. You tried the deviled eggs? You should try them."

When Benji finally stops to take a breath, I say, "I've got some matches in the emergency kit in my car."

He cocks his head like he's actually thinking about it. Then he shrugs. "They'd only bus us to some shittier school."

"Probably." Part of the reason Benji and I would have been a disaster couple was July. We were both friends with her, and forcing her to chose between us when we inevitably split would have been inhumane. The other reason is that he's got the personality of a bowl of warm grapes. "Ready for senior year?"

"Not really."

"Oh." I could try to slip away, but then I could wind up talking to some stranger who wants to know what I want to do with my life or where I'm planning to apply to college. The devil you know, you know? "So I hear you're doing *Hairspray* over at Truman."

"We are. July's a great Tracy." Benji stops and glances at me. "Was."

His bottom lip is trembling and he looks like he's going to cry, so I say, "Remember when she redid the songs from *Hairspray* so they were Harry Potter themed?"

"Good Morning, Voldemort!" Benji sings. A couple of people look our way, but I don't care.

"'Run and Spell That' was my favorite."

Benji wags a finger at me. "She finished the lyrics to 'Petunia, I'm a Wizard Now,' and they're hilarious."

"Wish I could've heard them."

My attempt to change the subject leaves us almost in the same place we started, but at least Benji doesn't look on the verge of tears anymore. We stand quietly for a moment. I'm about to claim the need to use the bathroom when he says, "You remember Zora Hood?"

I try not to tense, but my face goes rigid and I can't look Benji in the eye. "I know her."

"She was July's understudy." He pauses, bites his lip. "At the funeral she said she saw July driving your car last night, but then you showed up and said it wasn't her. That's silly, right?"

"We're at July's funeral, Benji. What do you think?" I have to get away from him, so I say, "If you'll excuse me." Without waiting for him to reply, I slide through the crowd, run up the stairs, and rush to July's room, shutting the door behind me.

"Hiding?"

Startled, I spin around. Joëlle is sitting at July's desk in front of her open laptop. She's wearing a black-and-gray checkered suit with an oversized bowtie and suspenders that's totally her. July used to complain because she'd wanted a sister she could play dress up with, but Jo refused to wear dresses or skirts.

"Kind of," I say.

"Let me guess: Uncle Stu pull out his big bag of offensive jokes on you?"

"No, but a woman named Gloria cornered me for a while. Someone should tell her that while bathing is good, bathing in perfume is not."

Jo wrinkles her nose, and in that moment she looks so much like July that it hurts. "Not sure I know her." She shakes her head. "There are so many people here I don't know."

I flop down on the bed and arrange July's pillows behind me. The way Jo's watching me, I freeze. "What?"

"Everyone else comes in here treating it like a museum. You're the first person who hasn't."

"Sorry," I stutter. "I didn't mean—"

"Doesn't bother me."

Now I feel awful, though. Her parents were probably keeping it enshrined in amber so they could come into this room and see it the way July had left it. Maybe I can fix the pillows the way they were.

"I'm serious," Jo says. "Relax. And take off your jacket, too. You're making everyone else look bad."

I grimace. "Can't. I forgot to wear an undershirt, and it was ridiculously hot out there today, so . . ."

Joëlle nods. "Got it. That'll make Logan and Trey feel better."

"Great, now I'm self-conscious about it."

"You should be." Her grin is pure July, but there's a warmth to her words that's all her own.

I motion at the computer. "Trying to hack her system?"

Jo nods. "I know she kept her diary on here, and I'm hoping it'll tell me how she used to sneak out without Mom knowing."

"That's easy," I say. "She wired the sensor for the back door so it always reads as active. I don't think it's worked since your mom had it installed."

"Very clever, July," Jo says.

"Yeah. Your sister was an evil genius."

Jo closes the laptop and then leans back in the chair. I wait for her to say something, but it seems like she's leaving it up to me to carry the conversation.

"Ready for high school?"

"No," Jo says emphatically.

"It won't be so bad. And you'll have at least one friend."

Joëlle pauses, then says, "We might not stay."

"At Palm Shores High?"

"In Palm Shores at all."

My eyebrows shoot up. "For real?"

"Mom's felt like the house was too big since Daddy left, and now with July gone, she's talking about moving closer to Grandma."

"Atlanta?"

Jo shakes her head. "She's in Colorado now."

I'm surprised Mrs. Cooper is considering leaving. Especially so soon. But I can also see how painful it would be staying in the space July had once filled and being constantly forced to remember she's never returning.

"What do *you* want?" I ask.

"Don't know."

"You seem to be holding up pretty well."

Jo grins. "You missed the meltdown I had this morning trying to get dressed. The remains of five shirts are still sitting on my floor, and my tablet's definitely toast." Her smile fades and she looks directly at me. "How are you doing it? Staying so calm, I mean?"

"July's not dead for me yet."

"I know what you mean," Jo says. I doubt she actually does, not in the same way, but I don't interrupt her. "I was in the shower two nights ago and there were no towels, and I yelled for July to get me one before I remembered she was gone."

Only, July's not gone. Maybe. I don't know. Either way, I can't tell Jo. Seeing her family has to be July's decision. "I should go." I stand and then try to arrange the pillows the way they were, but they're still a mess.

"Dino?"

"Yeah?"

"I don't think she was really mad at you."

"No?" I say. "She seemed pretty angry."

"Shoot, that's because she didn't know how to be angry at herself, so she took it out on everyone else."

I wave as I head for the door. "I hope I'll see you in school next year. And if you do decide to stay, let me know. I'll give you a ride."

"Thanks, Dino."

DINO

THE LAST PERSON I WANT TO SEE IS RAFI, BUT HE'S SITTING ON the patio steps at the front door when I pull into the driveway at my house. There's a cardboard box beside him. He looks considerably better than I feel. Then again, I doubt he had to get up after only four hours of sleep to go to a funeral for someone who may or may not be not-dead and texting me from inside of her buried coffin.

Rafi stands when I get out of the car, and I feel like the ground's dropped out from under me. He's wearing the shirt he was wearing when I first saw him, even though that was a year ago and it's too tight across the shoulders now, but there's a sadness in his eyes that hits me harder than I expected it to.

"Hey, Dino," he says.

I motion at the box. "Stop by to return the stuff I gave you?" My voice comes out defensive, though I don't mean for it to. I'm not certain I agree with Jo's theory that July was angry at me when she should have been angry at herself, but I understand the idea, because how can I possibly be mad at Rafi?

Rafi's face contorts with pain like I've knifed him. Then he shakes his head. "How was the funeral?"

"Depressing."

He moves like he's going to hug me, but stops himself. "I'm sorry."

"I don't mean to be a dick," I say. "But I'm exhausted, so why are you here?"

Rafi nods and picks up the box. He reaches inside and pulls out a light blue T-shirt. "This is from the fundraising marathon we ran together." He passes it to me. Then he pulls out a torn paper bracelet. "Midnight madness at the fair." The items keep coming. "The comic book you said would change my life, a list of the bands you made me listen to, a picture of you yelling at the religious nut who camped out in front of the community center."

I interrupt him. "Rafi, what is this?"

He stops. "Last night, you said you don't know who you are. And how can I possibly love you if you have no idea who you are?" He shoves the box at me. There are still tons more things in it. A dried carnation, a drawing I don't remember doing, a pack of silver markers. "These things are who you are. At least, they're who you are to me."

I take the box and hold it awkwardly, wishing I could throw it away. "And what if the person I showed you isn't real?"

"Then I'm an idiot," Rafi says. "But, I've seen videos of you acting, Dino, and you're not that good."

DINO

THE UPPER PORTION OF THE COFFIN FLIPS OPEN, AND July sits up and goes, "Ta-da!" while giving me actual jazz hands.

I lean the shovel against the dirt wall of the grave and help July out of the coffin.

"Why the hell are you still alive?"

July shrugs. "Insomnia?"

I have so many questions, but I'm standing at the bottom of a grave, dirty with sweat streaking my arms and legs, and I want to fill the hole and get the hell out of the cemetery as quickly as possible.

"Your mom sewed my butt shut!" July yells. "Did you know she was gonna to do that?"

I grimace. "Kind of?"

"I'm not even going to tell you where she stuffed cotton. You said they weren't going to do any of that stuff."

"I said they weren't going to embalm you. But there's still the chance of leakage, and your parents wanted an open casket, so . . ."

"You have no idea how humiliating that was."

"Can we . . . ?" I motion at the ladder. July climbs out and I follow, but as soon as I'm up, I round on her and say, "Why aren't you dead? What're we going to do now? And how did you get a phone?"

July scans the cemetery. There's plenty of moonlight, but I was too scared to bring a flashlight, so everything looks a little spooky. "You want to have this talk here? Now?"

"No, but we can't leave this giant hole here, and you might as well explain while we work."

July looks at me, then the shovel. "We?"

"Are you seriously not going to help?"

"Come on, Dino. A good friend will bury your body, but only a best friend will dig you back up and not make you help fill in the hole." She bats her eyelashes at me, and it's infuriating. But since I already have the blisters, I don't see any point in arguing. I pull the ladder out of the grave and begin shoveling dirt into it while July tells me what happened.

"I tried. I really did."

"Not hard enough," I mutter. Thankfully, filling a grave isn't nearly as exhausting as digging one, but it's still more manual labor than I'm used to, and there isn't a single muscle of mine that's not screaming in agony.

July ignores me. "It took me a while to work up the nerve, but I finally got on the gurney and went into the freezer."

"Weren't you cold?"

"No," she says, and there's a trace of sadness in her voice. "I shut my eyes and counted backward from one thousand. My body is dead, so I had this idea that the only thing keeping me animated was my mind, and that if I could let go, I'd die for real. It didn't work the way I planned."

"How so?" My questions are short because of the exertion of shoveling dirt.

July leans against a nearby headstone. "You know how you get when you can't stop thinking and your mind churns out scenarios? You finally come up with the perfect comeback to every insult flung at you since the dawn of time, and you go over every argument you've ever had or will ever have in the future? That's what happened to me."

"So you were awake for everything?" I ask. "My mom dressing you, the church service, the burial?"

"The whole sordid adventure."

"How did you not move?"

July chuckles. "Well, I may not have been able to fall asleep, but if I close my eyes and focus on my thoughts, I can blur out what's happening around me. I don't breathe and I don't feel much, so to an outsider I look completely dead. I did okay until Aunt Franny was standing over me, and she was making this big fuss—"

"I remember," I say. "'Blubbering' is a word that comes to mind."

"Franny never liked me, and I thought it was so hilarious that she was putting on such a show that I laughed. Barely. It was hardly even a snort."

"*That's* what happened! No one could figure out why she screamed and then took off."

July grins, looking pretty proud of herself. "After that, I was a lot more careful."

"But *why*?" I ask. "If you weren't dead, why didn't you call me? And you still haven't told me where you got a phone from."

"The phone's easy," July says. "It's mine. I stole it from my room when I snuck into my house." She holds the phone up so I can see it. "I would've called after my stupid plan failed, but I knew it would've caused a whole scandal if my body disappeared, so I decided to let the funeral happen. Plus, my battery died after I sent the selfies."

An involuntary shiver runs through me. "You let yourself be buried alive."

"Whatever. It wasn't so bad."

It's actually kind of sweet. July could have slipped away in the middle of the night and lived out the rest of her not-life somewhere else, but it would have been a disaster for my family. That she stayed means a lot to me.

I stop digging and lean against the shovel. "So what do we do now?"

"I honestly have no idea," July says. "But what's going on is bigger than me."

It takes me a couple of hours to fill the hole, and I'm exhausted by the time I pat down the last of the dirt. It doesn't look like it did when I got here, but I doubt anyone will suspect someone sneaked into the cemetery to dig up July. I hope.

"Come on," I say. "Let's go to my house. We'll figure this out in the morning."

July carries the shovel while I take the ladder. "Hey," she says. "At least I don't smell anymore."

"You still smell, July."

"You're an asshole."

"God, I wish you'd stay dead."

July nudges me with her shoulder and says, "Thanks for not leaving me down there."

"Don't get me wrong. I definitely considered it."

"Liar."

"And I'm already regretting it."

"Yeah," July says. "Me too."

JULY

DINO MUMBLES IN HIS SLEEP. GIGGLES TOO. IT'S NOT cute. When he does it, he sounds and looks like he's about to disembowel a room full of puppies. Creeped me out the first time he spent the night at my house. Momma had always known Dino was gay. She never said so, but that's the only reason that explains why she let a boy and girl have sleepovers together well into high school. That *should* have clued me in that Dino was different, but I didn't see it. I wasn't in love with him or anything like that. Dino was my partner in crime; the one person in the world I wanted to spend my life with. Sure, we could both get married and have kids and whatever, but at the end of our lives, I wanted it to be us and no one else. I guess I didn't expect our ends to happen so far apart.

After my unburial, I made Dino take me to the beach so I could set fire to the blue dress. It meant riding to his house and sneaking into his room in my skivvies, but it was so worth it. Thankfully, he kept the clothes I wore last night. I tried to convince Dino to stay awake with me, but he grumbled about four hours of sleep and crashed into his bed the second we got into his room.

During midterms and finals, I used to think it'd be great if I never had to sleep. I'd daydream about those extra hours I could have and all that I could do with them while the rest of the lazy world lay in their beds. The reality is that being awake while everyone else is asleep sucks. I kill time playing video games, and then I get this idea to research burial rituals to see if I can find information that might help me understand why I'm still not-dead and how to fix it. Some cultures used to eat their dead. I doubt Dino would be into that. The Malagasy people of Madagascar dig up the dead once every seven years, wrap the corpses in cloth, and dance with them. The practice sounds interesting, but I'm glad Dino didn't leave me buried for seven years. And the Zoroastrians had a complicated set of rites that involve bull urine, a holy dog, a tower, and vultures. I'm not even sure where I'd get bull pee. Even though none of this is offering me any solutions for my problem, I get lost in a clickhole until I stumble on a story from a news website.

"Dino!"

He snorts and rolls over, covering his face with his arm.

"It made the news," I say. "Get up."

"One night. I just want one night of sleep," Dino moans. "Is that too much to ask? One night where I don't have to babysit or dig up a corpse. Please?"

"Quit whining." I grab a book off his desk and toss it at him.

"Ow!" he says. "That was only my knee."

"And it was only a book. Not even a hardcover, so quit complaining."

Dino tosses aside his comforter and sits up. Wearing only boxers and socks, he looks so spindly and breakable, but, and I'll never tell him this, the boy's tougher than he appears.

"You have to see this," I say.

"Pee first, then talk." He disappears into the bathroom. I forgot how grumpy he is when he wakes up. I've got so many videos of him shambling through my house first thing in the morning with his eyes glued shut, stumbling into walls and trying not to stab anyone while my mom yammers at him. When I wake up, my brain and body fire from sleep to wake immediately, but Dino needs a solid hour to warm up before he's anywhere near coherent.

Dino returns ten minutes later with a glass of orange juice.

"Thought you were going to the bathroom?" I ask.

He glares at me and sits down in his bed with his juice, sipping it slowly. His eyes are only half-open, and his hair is an overgrown garden.

I doubt he's going to get any more receptive than this for a while, so I launch straight into it. "There's a story about how no one's dying."

"Okay."

"A nurse in Rhode Island was the first to notice it, so she called a couple of nearby hospitals, and it spread from there."

I check to make sure Dino's paying attention and hasn't fallen asleep again. He's a master at dozing with his eyes open. "Guess when the last death was?"

"The night you rose from the dead to torment me?" Dino says in a deeply annoyed monotone. The first fingers of light are crawling up the sky and brightening the room, but they only seem to darken Dino's mood.

"Correct. Best estimates place the last recorded death in Ankara, Turkey around the time I literally scared the piss out of you."

"I didn't *literally* wet my pants."

"Sure you did."

"I was wearing them. I'd remember."

"Whatever," I say. "In my memory of that moment, you were standing in a puddle."

Dino sips his OJ. "No surprise there. We've already proven your memory of events is basically crap."

"What's that—" I stop myself. Wag my finger at him. "Nope. You're not dragging me into a fight to avoid talking about this."

"Talking about what?"

"That the world is falling apart and it's my fault." I wait for some smartass retort, but he's got nothing to say. "Here's how I'm thinking about it: There are two possible explanations— well, there might be more, but I'm focusing on the two that make the most sense to me. The first is that something suspended death. Folks can't die anymore. As a side effect of that, I'm also not-dead, but not not-dead in the way that those others are. They can't die, but I was already dead. The second possibility is that somehow I returned from the dead, and in doing so short-circuited death itself, making it so that no one can die until I die. Again."

Dino got more sleep than he thinks, which left me with a lot of time to consider the various explanations.

"What about—"

"I'm not finished," I say. "Now, if the first explanation is true, why did it affect me? Shouldn't there be others like me waking up? Folks who are recently dead? Yes, there should be. But there aren't. You've got a fresh body in the freezer that hasn't so much as twitched a finger. I would know. I watched him for ten minutes before I got in there with him. So what's more likely: that some worldwide phenomenon suspended death and also returned to something-like-life one single corpse among the hundreds of billions of corpses buried on this planet, or that some miracle brought me back, which had the side-effect of pausing death for everyone else?"

Dino opens his mouth to speak, but closes it without a word. His eyes look a little wider, a little more alert, but he's still struggling through the morning fog in his brain. After a minute of quiet he says, "Actually, that makes sense."

"Ha!"

"Ha?"

"Told you the world revolved around me."

"Thank God I only have to hear you gloat about this for the rest of your not-life, which will hopefully be short."

I do a little dance in my chair. It's not particularly dignified, but I don't care.

"So what do we do?" Dino asks.

"Do?"

Dino shrugs. "If we assume that your reanimation is the cause of the . . ."

"Miracle."

"Really?"

"That's what they're calling it in the news," I say.

Dino raises his eyebrows and shakes his head. "Yeah, they won't be calling it that for long."

"Then let's use it ironically."

"I don't think—"

"I don't care."

Dino mumbles under his breath.

"What?"

Dino holds up his hands. Band-Aids cover the blisters. "I dug up your body, I'm in pain, I haven't slept in two days," he says. "And I'm having a rough morning. Where's the sympathy?"

For a second, I feel bad for him, but it passes. "When your mom sews your butt shut, then I'll feel sorry for you. Until then, you'll have to deal with it like the rest of us."

A whole range of emotions scrolls across Dino's face, and I can't decide whether he's wishing he could set me on fire or chop my pretty corpse into a hundred pieces and scatter them across Palm Shores. Good thing I didn't tell him about the vultures.

"Anyway," he says. "If we assume you're the cause of the *miracle*, what are we going to do about it?"

"Got me. I did my bit. Went into the freezer, had a funeral, got buried."

"How was that, by the way?" he asks.

"Which part?"

"The funeral." He's pursing his lips in that serious way of his.

I shut the laptop to give him my full attention. "It was okay, I guess. That priest was boring, but the music was nice." I stare down my nose at Dino. "Though I noticed a certain someone didn't bother eulogizing my magnificence."

Dino bows his head. "I couldn't."

"Too overcome with grief?"

"You're not-dead!"

"That's a terrible excuse."

Dino sets his mostly-empty glass of juice on his nightstand. "You always do this."

"Do what?"

"Change the subject. Every time I bring up a topic you don't want to talk about, you turn it into a joke or a fight or you storm off to 7-Eleven and almost get arrested."

"Oh my God," I say. "That happened once. Get over it."

"Two nights ago!" He growls. "See? You're doing it again."

I clench my fists. "What do you want from me, Dino? You want me to tell you it was torture lying in that coffin, listening to Momma and Daddy crying, to Jo thanking people for coming to watch me get buried, thinking the whole time that I could sit up and take away their pain, but that if I did so I might only be setting them up to get hurt later?"

"I want to know how you feel," Dino says. "To know that you *can* feel."

"Of course I feel. I feel everything since I woke up staring at your ugly face. Some of the time I'm terrified that I'm going to be stuck this way forever. That I'm going to bloat and rot and then that my skin and insides will wither until I'm a husk, but that I still won't die. That a thousand years from now, future humans will be zipping through the sky in flying cars with their cloned dinosaur pets, taking vacations on the moon, and I still won't be dead, but that I won't be alive either."

Dino clears his throat. "They won't have cloned dinosaurs. There isn't enough DNA for—"

I cut him off with a single sharp glance. "But most of the time I'm scared about my folks and Jo. Not that they won't be okay without me—they will be, I know they will—but that they're going to move on and forget me."

"You know they won't," Dino says.

"Maybe not completely," I say. "But Joëlle's their only daughter now. She's the one they'll watch graduate, the one they'll walk down the aisle, the one they'll worry over and fuss about and show pictures of to their friends. Jo is the future, full of potential. I'm nothing but the past. Painful memories they can visit if they want to. But why would they look back when Jo's giving them so much to look forward to?"

Dino folds his hands and avoids looking at me. "July . . ."

"And you know what the worst part is? I can't even cry about it. I can't squeeze out one single tear for the life I'm leaving behind or the shitshow I've got to look forward to."

"Why didn't you tell me you felt like this before?"

I laugh bitterly. "I wanted to tell my best friend, but we haven't been that to each other in a long time."

DINO

"I NEED A SHOWER," I SAY. "WHEN I'M DONE, WE'LL FIGURE out what to do next." I barely make it to the bathroom, shut the door behind me, and crank on the water before I lose it. My whole body shakes. I sit on the floor with my knees pulled to my chest and tremble uncontrollably like I have a fever. My stomach roils and the pressure in my head is unbearable. It's too much. July dying and then coming back and then fake re-dying and making me dig her up; Rafi telling me he loves me, and me dumping him and not knowing whether I did the right thing. My sister's impending wedding and the stress of my parents' expectations for the future. I can't handle any of it. I feel like someone's torn me in half and is trying to jam the pieces together, but they don't fit anymore, so I'm just broken forever.

And then it passes. The shaking stops, the headache eases. Steam has filled the bathroom by the time the aftershocks subside.

I climb into the shower on autopilot. I showered when I got home from digging up July, but I don't think it's possible to fully wash the stink of grave robbing away. It's only when I grab the bar of soap that I realize I'm still wearing my boxers and socks. I peel them off and wring them out and toss them on the bath mat.

I am in control again. But I feel like I'm one shove from falling at any minute.

I've got to figure out what to do about July. The idea that she's causing people to not die is ludicrous, yet I can't fault her logic. Besides, it doesn't matter. We need to find a solution for *her*. If it happens to fix the *miracle*, great. If not, then the two incidents were never connected and it's not my problem. Except, I have no clue what caused July to return from the dead, and no plan for how to help her die for real.

July already attempted the simplest and most obvious solution. She closed her eyes and tried to will herself dead. Clearly she failed, though success was a long shot at best. It's possible if we burned her body and scattered the ashes, that would solve the problem, but not only does the thought of doing that to her freak me out, but I keep thinking about the woman missing a chunk of her brain. What if some part of July survived being burned? What if, instead of freeing her, I simply divided her into countless tiny pieces and tossed them to the wind, leaving her aware somehow, yet unable to act or speak?

No. Whatever we decide will not involve harm to July's body. I don't care if I have to live with her rotting corpse for the rest of my life.

Logically, there's no scientific reason why July should be not-dead. I can't think of a single rational explanation for why she returned. But I can think of one very nonscientific, irrational reason. It's pretty unlikely, but it's all I've got.

Excited to tell July, I get out of the shower, wrap a towel around my waist, and burst into my room. "I have an idea."

"Oh, Dino! It's so nice to see you!"

"Grandma?"

Grandma Sue beams at me. She's short with silver hair that she always wears in intricate braids, and she's dressed in a pink blouse tucked into high-waisted mom jeans. She moves fast for someone her age, and she's on me with hugs before I can retreat.

"Don't," I say. "I'm wet."

"Please," she says. "You could be covered in mucus, and I'd still take a hug." Grandma pulls away and pokes me in the stomach. "Your mother's not feeding you enough."

Keeping one hand firmly on the towel, I use the other to fend her off. There's nothing I hate more than being body shamed by my grandmother before breakfast.

"What're you doing here?" I covertly look for July but don't see her anywhere.

"Is that how you greet your grandmother?"

"Sorry," I say. "No. I know you're here for the wedding, but I thought you weren't coming in until later. And how'd you get in? My door was locked."

Grandma toddles to my bed, where she's spread her suitcase open and is already making herself at home. "I was visiting Dixie in Clermont and I woke up early this morning, excited to see my delightful grandchildren—" She throws the last bit over her shoulder with a grim smile. "So I got on the road early. As for the door . . ."

Dee pops her head in the room. "Good, you're up. Grandma's going to be staying in your room. I let her in while you were in the shower."

"Thanks for the head's up."

"Put on some clothes for God's sake."

Grandma Sue chuckles. "Oh, please. I used to bathe him in the kitchen sink."

My face is burning. "Please kill me."

"Well," Dee says, "I doubt much has changed."

"Out!" I shove Dee into the hall. Then I turn to Grandma and say, "Hey, would you mind letting me have the room for a few minutes? I need to get dressed and get my things so I don't bother you while you're here."

Grandma looks at her suitcase. "Well, I was going to take a nap—"

"You know what I'd love? Some of your lemon ricotta pancakes."

"You're hungry?"

I nod. "Mom doesn't usually cook breakfast, so—"

That's all it takes. Grandma pats my cheek and heads for the door. "Give me fifteen minutes and I'll whip up a little snack." Translated from grandma means she's going to tear apart the kitchen making enough food to feed Hannibal's army, which is exactly what I need.

The moment she's gone, I shut the door, lock it, and whisper, "July?" My heart begins to sputter. "July?"

My closet door cracks open slightly. "Is she gone?"

Relief floods through me. "Yeah, she's gone. For now."

July stumbles out of the closet and slaps my arm.

"What was that for?"

"Why didn't you tell me she was coming?"

"I didn't know!"

July cocks her head and stares down at me. "You didn't know?"

"Okay, I knew she was going to be here eventually, but I didn't know she was going to show up at seven in the morning." The reality of how close we came to my grandma finding July hits me, and I have to sit on my bed, because I feel like I'm going to pass out. "What're we going to do?"

July holds her hands over her eyes. "You're going to put on some underwear to start."

I snap my legs closed, then jump up and dig a clean pair of boxers, a shirt, and gym shorts out of my drawer and quickly change. "Done."

July glances my way like she doesn't trust I'm not going to still be naked. She looks relieved to see I'm clothed. Which makes two of us. "How are you going to get me out of here?"

"The window?"

"We're on the second floor," she says. "And you saw how easy my thumb came off. What happens if I fall and break a bone? Doubt it'll heal."

"Good point."

"Well?" July says. "Hurry up and think. I can't stay in your closet forever."

Lack of sleep is making everything difficult. There are so many thoughts in my brain, and I can't process them. "Okay. Fine. We're going to have to sneak you into the office until we find a more permanent hiding place."

July doesn't look impressed with my plan and, to be fair, it isn't so much a plan as it is the only idea I could come up with in under a minute.

"Follow me," I say.

I poke my head out my door and peer down the hallway. Mom and Dad's bedroom door is open, and their bed is made, which is usually a sign they've gone to the kitchen for breakfast. Dee's door is shut, but I'm betting she's still with Grandma.

I wave July on, and we make for the stairs. I pause when I reach the bottom, and July stops on the landing.

"It smells god-awful in there." Grandma's voice drifts in amid the sounds of sizzling butter and clanking pans. "Does Jennifer ever clean?"

"Jenn and I both do the cleaning, Mom, but Dino is old enough to be responsible for his own room. I'll have him clean it today."

"No, no. I'll take care of it," Grandma says. "Speaking of Dino, where is he? Delilah, tell your brother breakfast is nearly ready."

The sound of a chair scraping against the tile sends a chill down my spine. *"Run!"* I whisper to July, and she stumbles while turning and has to claw herself to her feet. She's not going to make it so I rush to the end of the stairs and plow into Dee, nearly taking us both down.

"Jesus, Dino, what's the rush?" She glares at me and pushes me off.

"Smelled the bacon."

"Good," she says, though she still sounds annoyed. "Grandma says it's ready." She moves to walk past me, and I stick my arm out to lean against the wall and block her path.

"Aren't you hungry?"

"I'm not eating so much as a carrot between now and tomorrow. My wedding dress fits perfectly, and I refuse to mess that up over a stack of pancakes."

"You can't seriously expect the grandparents to let you not eat. The rehearsal dinner's tonight."

Dee shoves me aside, rolling her eyes. "I don't have time for you this morning, Dino." She stomps up the stairs, disappears into her room, and slams the door. A few seconds later, July's head pops around the corner. I wave at her, and she rushes down the stairs.

If death weren't suspended, the stress of this would kill me. I reach the front door and hold it open for July to stealthily dash through. The biggest problem is that the kitchen window looks across the lawn, but there's no way to avoid that. I have to hope no one's standing at the sink when we make a break for it.

My hands tremble with the keys at the office door, but I open it and stand aside to let July in. I'm about to follow her when a voice stops me.

"Dino?"

Mom's standing at the corner of the far side of the office, holding one hand behind her back. She doesn't speak for a second, but then she blows out a mouthful of smoke that drifts on the air and disappears.

I let the door swing shut and then slip my keys into my pocket. "Are you smoking?"

Sheepishly, Mom brings out her hand and holds the lit cigarette in front of her. "What are you doing?" Her deflection makes me smile. Of all my mom's rebellions, it's the smoking she's embarrassed about. Which, yeah, I don't like it, but it's nice to know she's not perfect.

"Uh . . . looking for the portable fan," I say. "You know how Grandma Sue's perfume gets to my head. I checked the garage, and I thought I'd look in the office." It's a passable lie, and I'm actually pretty proud of myself for thinking so quickly on my feet.

Mom nods. "Sorry about Sue. She showed up this morning without warning and called your father to say she was outside." She pauses. "Were you having nightmares? I heard you talking to yourself when I got up."

"Yeah," I say. "Lots of dreams. Don't remember them." I quickly change the subject. "Are you hiding?"

"I was inside balancing the books, if you must know." She holds my eyes for a full ten seconds before breaking down and saying, "Fine, I'm hiding." She clenches her fists and her temples pulse in and out. "I am forty-four years old and that woman still makes me feel like I'm sixteen. She never wanted me to work with your father even though I'm ten times better at it than he is. And she thinks I should spend my time cooking and cleaning and taking care of you kids."

Mom puffs hard on the cigarette; the cherry flares like the sun.

"You do," I say. "You're the most organized mom I know. And unlike most of the families in Palm Shores, you do it without a maid service."

Mom laughs at that. "Trust me, if we could afford it . . ."

"No way," I say. "Dad would go behind them and reclean whatever they did."

"You're not wrong." Mom finishes the cigarette, stubs it out against the side of the office, and slips the butt in her pocket. "Not to pry," she says. "But I saw Rafi yesterday when he came by to wait for you. Is everything okay?"

I don't want to talk to my mom or anyone about my breakup, but if I don't tell her something, she'll turn it around in her brain until she makes a bigger deal out of it than it is. "We broke up."

"Any particular reason?" She may be acting cool, but she's dying to ask a million questions.

"He told me he loved me, and I couldn't say it back."

Mom bites the inside of her lip, which is usually a sign that she's on the verge of lecturing me on how badly I've screwed up my life. Somehow she manages to resist the impulse. "I worry about you, Dino."

"Me? Why?"

"I don't want you to get so caught up trying to protect yourself from getting hurt that you miss out on life."

"Trust me," I say. "Breaking up with Rafi was for the best. He deserves to be happy."

"So do you."

"I know."

"Are you? Happy, I mean?"

"Not yet. But I'm working on it."

Mom nods. "Good enough." She rubs my cheek and smiles. "I think I saw the fan in the shed. But don't take too long looking. If your grandmother is doting on you, she's not picking on me."

"I'll hurry," I say. "Promise."

JULY

"I COULD BE YOUR DATE TO THE WEDDING," I SAY. AFTER Dino left me to go have breakfast, I made myself at home as best I could in one of the top-of-the-line coffins until he returned a couple of hours later. The lining is satin and padded. The only luxury missing is a mini bar. I should design my own line of coffins for people who are buried not-dead.

Dino's sitting on a folding chair. His body is tense, but I can't tell what's on his mind. He's been preoccupied since this morning. "There aren't enough prosthetics in the office for that."

"What's wrong with my face?"

"With the layers of makeup you keep slathering on, you're starting to look like drag Dolly Parton."

"See!" I say. "How is it okay for you to make a drag queen joke, but when I made a gay joke at Rafi's house, his friends went batshit on me?"

Dino stops jiggling his leg. "What did you say?"

"Not important. Answer the question."

"You didn't earn it," Dino says.

I stare down my nose at him. From up here, I feel like I'm on a raised dais atop my throne. "And you did with all the drag shows you've performed in?"

"Okay," he says. "No. But I also wasn't making fun of drag culture. I was making fun of Dolly Parton, which, come to think of it, isn't cool either." He shakes his head. "Look at it this way: How would you feel if I made a joke about women being crappy drivers?"

"Considering the way you drive, I'd definitely punch you."

"As a woman, you could make that joke if you wanted to," he goes on. "Since I'm a part of gay culture, I can joke about it if I want. You can't because you're not gay."

"Just gay adjacent."

Dino laughs quietly. "Rafi hates those kinds of jokes. He says jokes that rely on demeaning a marginalized group, even if they're made by a person from within that group, show a lack of respect. He believes jokes can be painful but that they shouldn't hurt."

"How does that make sense?" I ask.

"Humor can shine a light on truths that make us uncomfortable, and we all know how painful facing the truth is, but that humor doesn't have to come from another person or group's pain." Dino shrugs. "Anyway, Rafi thinks I make jokes to cover how deeply uncomfortable I am with myself."

"He's got a point," I say.

Instead of answering, Dino stands and starts pacing a line in front of the coffin displays. "I have a theory about why you're not-dead," he says. "It came to me in the shower, but then I didn't get the chance to tell you because—"

"Invasion of Grandma."

"Exactly."

I sit up a little more and give Dino my full attention. "So what is it? Alien meteor from space? Secret government serum? Dark magic?"

"Me."

My mouth is open and I'm laughing before I realize I'm doing it. It's involuntary, and once I start, I can't stop. "Oh good," I say. "I'm so glad you've finally recovered your sense of humor."

Dino stops pacing and turns his somber face in my direction. "I'm not joking."

"Come on," I say. "You think you're the reason I'm not-dead?"

"Us, really."

"Us?"

Dino nods and then returns to his pacing. "Think about it. What's the one part of your life you left unfinished by dying suddenly?"

I count them off on my fingers. "High school, my relationship with Jo, the summer musical, *The Break Up Protection Program*, a dozen different book series and TV shows—"

"I get it," he says. "But how important are those?"

"Pretty damn important."

"Why does graduating matter if you're not going to be alive

to go to college? You've got an understudy for the musical." July scowls when I mention Zora, but I quickly keep going. "I talked to Jo after the funeral, and she's messed up now, but I think she's going to be okay eventually. I told her how you fixed the alarm so you could sneak out."

I grin because I'm pretty proud of that one. Momma never knew, and now Jo can use it too. "That's fine, but I wish I could tell her all the crap I've learned directly instead of hoping she'll hack my computer and read my diary."

"She'll figure it out," Dino says. "You said it yourself. Your family's going to be hurting for a long time, but they're strong. They'll survive."

"Whereas, without me you'll spend the rest of your life wallowing in guilt for not appreciating me and for ditching me to be with a guy you broke up with the day before my funeral, and will end up a lonely alcoholic working at a job you hate and spending your nights thinking of the things you wished you'd said to me when I was still alive?"

Dino snorts and stumbles. "Yeah, I was thinking more like the giant rift in our friendship is what's keeping you from staying dead."

"Do you honestly think you were that important to me?"

"You could have woken up while you were still in your house, before the paramedics arrived, in the morgue, in the freezer before I pulled you out. But you didn't. You woke up in my parents' funeral home, with me." He shrugs. "I think that's got to mean something."

"Yeah," I say. "It means you're annoying enough to wake the dead."

"I'm trying to be serious."

"No you're not," I tell him. "Not if you honestly think I'm going to believe that our broken friendship is the obstacle keeping me from resting in peace."

Dino throws up his hands in frustration. "What else could it be then? Go on, July. Tell me what else could have caused what we've been through."

"I just did!"

"Because you might miss some TV shows? I'm sure they'll have Netflix in heaven."

"So you think I'm going to heaven?"

"No," he says. "But I'm sure hell has Hulu."

The muscles in Dino's jaw are pulsing. He's going to grind his teeth to crumbles soon. "Fine," I say. "Let's pretend for a second that you're right." It's difficult to say without laughing. "And that I'm not-dead because you're a dick who ruined our friendship. How do we fix it?"

Dino closes his eyes and takes a deep breath. "You can begin by not calling me names, and maybe by accepting that you are also to blame for what happened."

"Now you're really talking nonsense."

"Should *I* make a list? Didn't we already go over some of the ways you screwed up?"

Yeah, this isn't funny anymore. I cross my arms over my chest and glare at Dino. "What? Like the Halloween party? Pushing Anya in the pool?"

"That's one," Dino says. "There are plenty more."

"So the way you remember that night is that I was so jealous of you for spending time talking to a girl who wasn't me, that I shoved her into the pool? Correct?"

"Pretty much," he says. "Though you forgot the time between arriving at the party and the shove heard 'round the patio, where you stood to the side glaring at her, me, and everyone who came near me."

I'm clenching my fists so tightly I'm afraid I'm going to tear my skin again, and I have to force myself to relax. "Let me tell you about Anya. You went inside to use the bathroom, and I thought I'd chat her up and see what her deal was. Get to know her. I introduced myself and told her I was your friend and said how great you were, and Anya, with her fake-ass British accent, told me she was always looking for another fag to add to her collection."

"She did not."

"She did."

"But I wasn't even out yet." Some of his anger vanishes.

"Oh, Dino, that's so cute that you thought it wasn't obvious to anyone with eyes."

Dino trudges toward the coffin and leans against the closed end near my legs. "That's why you pushed her?"

I'd be blushing so hard if I could. "Mostly."

"There's more?"

"Yeah," July says. "So she made the comment about you and I called her a bitch, and then she asked me if I worried about whalers when I went to the beach, so I shoved her pretentious ass into the water." I pause. "As for the hours of glares before-hand . . ." I shrug. "I had cramps, I wanted to go home, and I was annoyed you'd talked me into coming. Nothing sinister there."

Dino's not looking at me. His eyes are unfocused and distant. He's likely replaying that night in his head, looking for what he missed. "You didn't tell me," he says.

"I would have if I'd known you'd been stewing about it this whole time. She said something shitty about you and then about me, I took care of her, and I didn't think about it much after that. Besides, you weren't out yet. You didn't need some uppity fake Brit messing with your head."

"But still," Dino says. "Why didn't you tell me? It would have cleared up so much."

"I guess I didn't think I needed to," I say. "I thought you knew I'd never intentionally hurt you." I sit quietly for a few moments unsure what's going through Dino's mind. Then I say, "Still not-dead. Guess your theory was wrong."

Dino looks up. "Fuck you, July."

"I'm pretty sure Death already has."

DINO

REGARDLESS OF WHAT JULY BELIEVES, I STILL THINK I'M the reason she's not-dead. That it's our friendship she can't let go of. If it were her parents and Jo, she'd be annoying them instead of me. I'm not discounting their pain, but they got as much closure as they're going to get. They know why July died and that there was nothing they could have done to prevent it. They had a beautiful funeral and got to say good-bye, and July even occupied the coffin of honor for it. If there are any unresolved issues there, I don't know what they are.

But our friendship has been the centerpiece of both of our lives for years. Before we stopped speaking, I'd have had a difficult time recalling a single memory that didn't involve July Cooper in some way. I kind of figured July and I would be together until the end. Even when I was with Rafi, and July was giving me the evil eye in the hallway between classes or across the cafeteria during lunch, there was a tiny part of me that believed we'd find our way back to one another. I think July must have too, and that she actually returned from death and is keeping everyone else in the world from dying until we finish this.

The problem is that July also may be correct that our friendship is beyond repair. Maybe there's just no way out of the boxes we've forced each other into.

I don't know. It's a lot to think about, and thinking is pretty difficult squeezed between Theo's younger brother, Will, and Grandpa Karl. None of us are particularly comfortable at the big round table outside on the patio at Loggerheads for Delilah and Theo's rehearsal dinner, but at least the view of the ocean is nice, and it's finally starting to cool down now that the sun is setting.

Theo and Dee are sitting across from me, and I can't tell whether my sister's enjoying herself or praying to every god she knows the name of that she not throw up. She flags down the waitress for another drink.

"Do you think that's a good idea, Delilah?" Grandma Sue asks.

"Probably not," Dee says at the same time as I say, "How do you expect her not to drink surrounded by this group? Hell, I've got a flask in my car."

The joke earns me some laughter, but Mom and Dad glare at me sharply. "You'd better not have," Dad says.

I hold up my hands. "Kidding, kidding." Then I start to stand. "Be right back."

Theo awkwardly high-fives me across the table, while most

of the adults stare down their noses in disapproval. We haven't been here long, but the conversation has ebbed and flowed in a natural way. Sometimes the entire table is involved, sometimes people break off into smaller pockets. I do feel slightly bad for abandoning July in the funeral home, but it's nice to talk about something other than her or us or death. I've spent so much of the last two days connected at the hip with my not-dead ex–best friend that it began to feel normal and I forgot what normal is supposed to feel like.

I think it's supposed to feel like this. Maybe. Normal is relative. And stupid.

"So you're a senior, Dino?" Mr. Kang asks. Dee and Theo are showing the grandparents pictures of their new house, which is actually pretty nice, so no one's paying attention to me.

"This year," I say.

"You must be excited," Mrs. Kang says.

I offer a smile with my shrug. "I guess."

Will elbows me. "Senior year is such a breeze. Take a bunch of electives and slide by." Theo's brother is a year older than me, but he's got a baby face that makes him look two years younger.

Mrs. Kang purses her lips. "Not everyone is content to *slide by*." She turns to me. "Your parents say you're very good at science."

"I'm okay. I think I like it more than I'm good at it."

"What will you study in college?" Mr. Kang asks.

"Everything?" I say with a laugh. "I'm kind of a dilettante. I get hyperfocused on a subject for a while, learn as much as I can about it, and then get bored and drop it."

Grandma Sue leans forward. "Don't be ridiculous. You're going to become a mortician like your father and sister."

"And mother," Delilah adds, but then she mouths *sorry* when I throw her an evil look.

"Do you want to be a mortician?" Mr. Kang asks. "I admit to not knowing much about the business, but it sounds intriguing."

Both Grandma Sue and Dad look like they're going to fight to see who can speak first, but thankfully the servers arrive with our dinners, and the conversation dies. Loggerheads is a seafood place, so there's a lot of snapper and lobster and tuna. I ordered a burger. I'm peeling back the bun to remove the pickles when Grandma Sue starts up again.

"No offense to Delilah, but DeLuca and Son's doesn't exist without a son."

"Names can be changed," Delilah says.

Dad covers his mouth with his napkin while he finishes chewing before he says, "You should have seen the work he did on his best friend. It was a beautiful job." He looks at me. "Did I tell you how many people complimented us on how July looked?"

Mrs. Kang says, "Your friend died? I'm so sorry for your loss."

"I told you about that, Ma," Theo says, and there's an edge to his voice hinting that he'd asked her not to bring it up.

"It's fine," I say. "Yeah. She died. Brain aneurism."

There's a moment of awkward silence, broken by Will, of all people. "How you planning to stay in business if no one's dying? You heard about that, right? I read on reddit about this dude who was cleaning his gun and shot himself in the eye and is still alive. He can't talk or feed himself or wipe his own butt—"

"William!" Mr. Kang says.

"What?"

Mom cuts in with, "Can we change the subject, please? This is Delilah and Theo's rehearsal dinner, not Dino's inquisition."

But it's too late. Even though they're trying not to stare, I feel everyone's eyes on me. Dino DeLuca, the Great Disappointment. "Excuse me," I say. "Restroom."

I stand and head along the edge of the patio toward the restrooms. As I'm walking, a hand snaps out and grabs me and yanks me into a booth. I turn to ask what the hell is going on, and find myself looking at July.

JULY

"THE SERVICE HERE SUCKS," I SAY. NOT THAT IT MATTERS, seeing as I can't eat or drink, but what does a not-dead girl have to do to get a server's attention?

Dino sputters and then looks over his shoulder.

"They can't see us," I say. "The booth blocks the view. But I can hear most of what's going on. Time to stand up for yourself, Dino. Tell them the only corpse you're spending the rest of your life with is mine."

"What are you doing here?" Dino asks when he finally finds his voice. "Better yet: *How* did you get here."

I tear strips off my napkin and twist them to keep from biting my nails because that thing about how fingernails and hair keep growing after you die is bullshit. "It took me a while to figure out you'd abandoned me. At first I got pissed. Then I got bored. Which lead to me getting nosy. I may have snuck up to the house and eavesdropped at the kitchen window—"

"July!"

"And overheard you getting ready to leave for the rehearsal dinner. So I hid in your trunk." I try to look sorry, but I'm not. "It's almost as comfortable as my coffin. Not that I'm saying I'd ride there voluntarily—again—but if you ever kidnapped me, I wouldn't complain. About the comfort, not about being kidnapped. I'd totally kick your ass for that."

I think I've broken Dino. He's staring at me with his mouth open, and I don't think he's blinked in a full minute. I snap my fingers in front of his face. "Dino?"

"This is a nightmare," he says. "You can't stay here."

"Seriously, why did your sister pick this place? There are a million better restaurants in Palm Shores."

"Because they're not rich," he snaps. "Dee and Theo are paying for their wedding with no help from either of their parents."

"Calm down. I was only kidding."

Dino scrubs his face with his hand and lets out a frustrated sigh. "Please leave, okay? Go wait in the car, and we'll talk about this when I'm finished."

I give him the finger with my eyes. "Or, I'll stay and enjoy the view and listening to you not tell everyone the truth."

"Which is?"

"That you're good at putting makeup on dead people, but that you hate it and want no part of the family business," I say.

"You're not confused; you're not still trying to figure it out. Not wanting to work at the funeral home may be the one thing you know for certain in your entire weird life."

"And I guess I'm supposed to say it exactly like that?"

I shrug. "Maybe with less sarcasm." I shoo him out of the booth. "You better go or everyone's going to assume you've been doing number two."

Dino gives me a mean stare, but slides out of the booth without another word and heads back to his table.

I do feel bad making fun of this restaurant now that I know Delilah's paying for it. I should have guessed she'd go that route, though. It's totally a Dee move, and I admire the hell out of her for it.

"Are you ready to order?" My server finally stops by my table. He's an older man with receding hair and razor burn across his cheeks and neck. He's holding his finger under his nose.

"Finally," I say. "I'll take the shrimp macaroni and cheese." I hand him the menu. "Throw some bacon in there too." I may not be able to eat the food, but I can't sit here at an empty table. The server nods and leaves.

I lean back as far as I can to see what I can hear at Dino's table. The other guests have gotten louder, and I wish they would shut up. I'm not familiar with everyone. There's Delilah, obviously. Theo, Mr. and Mrs. DeLuca, Grandma Sue. I assume the other old people are Dino's other grandparents. Then there's not-Theo, who looks a little like Theo if Theo had been an idiot burnout, and the people I'm assuming are Theo's parents.

"It's a mistake," Mr. DeLuca is saying. "People die. It's the only true certainty in life."

"So then it's a hoax?" probably Theo's mom says.

"It must be."

Not-Theo says, "How cool would it be if no one died? Like, we'd all keep living forever."

"It'd be less cool than you think," Mrs. DeLuca adds. "Unless you like overpopulation, resource shortages, territory wars. Basically the worst disaster in human history."

Ha! I knew I was right about that overpopulation scenario, but it's weird how oddly excited Dino's mom sounded describing that stuff.

Delilah clears her throat. "While I would love to continue discussing funerals and death, let's not. At least until after the wedding." Dino could learn a few things from his sister about being direct. She goes on to thank them for being there and helping her and for not shipping her to Australia when she lost her mind a little during the planning. Boring stuff.

I turn in the booth and peek around the corner to see if I can catch a glimpse of Dino. He's sitting at the table like he's got a titanium spine. Eyes deader than mine, vacant, staring straight ahead. He hasn't touched his burger.

A shadow falls over my table, and someone clears their throat. My server is standing over me, and he's not carrying food.

"Did you run out of shrimp?" I ask.

He keeps his voice low when he speaks, like he's telling me a secret. "There's been a complaint from some other customers."

His eyes dart to the booth across from mine, and he's looking at me meaningfully like I'm supposed to know what the hell he's hinting at. "About the smell?"

Oh. Yeah. The stink of me slowly putrefying. Got it. "Well," I say, in an equally conspiratorial tone. "We are near the ocean."

"I don't think—"

"Are you insinuating that the smell is coming from me?"

"No, but—"

"Accusing me of—" I stop myself. No. This is not okay. This guy knows I'm the source of the smell, and I can't lie and try to convince him I'm not. I wave him a little nearer. "You're right. It's me. I . . . I had a surgery. The smell is a side effect." I can't blush, so I bite my lower lip and look down. "I haven't left my house in weeks because I can't control the . . ." I lower my voice to barely above a whisper. "*The gas*. But I was feeling claustrophobic, and I wanted dinner at my favorite restaurant even though I knew I shouldn't have come." I scoot toward the end of the booth. "I'm so sorry. I'll leave."

Okay, so I traded one lie for another, but at least this lie doesn't paint anyone other than me in a negative light. And as I lay it out, the hardness melts from his eyes, replaced by sympathy. My waiter shakes his head firmly. "You stay and enjoy your meal. I apologize for bothering you." He walks away and I hear him at the next table saying, "These kinds of smells come from the ocean sometimes. May I offer you a table inside?"

Before I can bask in the glory of my victory, Dino slides into my booth. "I can't do this," he says.

"Do what?"

"Tell them."

"They already know."

Dino bows his head. "No they don't," he says. "I've talked around it, hoping they'd get the hint, but I've never come straight out and said it." He glances at me. "Besides, this night is supposed to be about Delilah. I'd be a jerk if I made it about me."

"That's never stopped you before."

My waiter shows up with my meal, eyes Dino curiously, and leaves.

"You ordered dinner?" Dino says. "But you can't eat."

The rounded backs of pink shrimp poke out of the surface of bubbling cheesy goodness, and there are chunks of brown bacon swirled within. I put my nose as near to the dish as I can and suck air into my chest cavity. The savory aroma is muted, like when I'd catch a cold and my nose would get stuffed, but I can almost smell the richness of the bacon, the sweetness of the shrimp. It's all tinged with a sour, rotten edge, but I remember how these foods are supposed to smell, and for now, it's enough.

"Look," I say when I'm done sniffing my dinner. "Have you learned nothing from the last two days with me?"

Dino rolls his eyes. "Oh, I've definitely learned some things. None of which will help me now, though."

"Be honest," I say. "Don't sugarcoat it, don't dance around it. Tell the truth and stand your ground."

"You think that'll work?"

"Yes!"

"I'll try, but you know how they are."

"I also know how *you* are." I point at him. "So don't be you. Be me. Okay?"

Dino nods. "Okay."

As he slides out of the booth, I grab his arm. "Before you go. Got any cash? I left my wallet in the coffin."

DINO

MOM TILTS HER HEAD AND SMILES TIGHTLY AT ME. "YOU okay, Dino? I've got some stuff in my purse if your stomach is upset."

Everyone at the table is pretending to ignore my mom subtly asking me if I've got diarrhea, and I'm grateful for the distraction. Most of the conversation is focused on Dee and Theo's honeymoon, which is a six-week trip to Europe.

"It's killing Delilah to not have everything planned," Theo says. "We have our plane tickets to London, two nights in the city, a train ticket to anywhere, and nothing else."

Dee slaps his arm. "It is not killing me." Then she turns to his parents and mouths, *It's totally killing me.*

Everyone calls out their favorite destinations as the servers clear the dinner plates. Grandma Jodi's vote is for Dublin, and then she launches into a story about a young man she met while she was there the summer before college, which is a story I guess Grandpa Karl's never heard, judging by his red-faced scowl. Mrs. Kang thinks Budapest, while Mr. Kang offers Venice. Will calls out Bangkok and then spends ten minutes giggling. And Grandma Sue tries to tell them they should stay in their own country because there's no place more wonderful than home, but everyone ignores her. I don't offer any suggestions. Dee had a map tagged with all the places in the world she wanted to visit long before she met Theo, so she may not have the tickets, but I guarantee she knows where she's going.

I could let them keep talking for the rest of the night. Stuff my face with little cakes or whatever is for dessert, slip away, and not have to deal with this. Until the next time it comes up. When I begin my senior year, when it's time to apply to college, when I choose a college and declare a major. And if I keep ignoring it, eventually I'm going to look up and find myself staring at a dead body because I'll have become my sister or my parents without realizing it. I want to choose my future, not settle for it.

"I'm not going to be a mortician," I say. At first, I don't think anyone hears. Delilah is the only person who looks at me. But then my mom and dad stop talking, and soon everyone is watching me, waiting to see what absurd words fly out of my mouth next.

Dad says, "Let's talk about this later."

Delilah shakes her head. "It's okay. Say what you need to say, Dino."

I glance toward July's booth, expecting to see the back of her head, leaning ever so slightly toward our table so she can hear better, but she's gone. With everyone looking at me now, I try to think of what to say next. No. I try to think of what July would say next.

"Look, I'm glad you love dead people so much, but I don't. I'm not interested in spending the rest of my life living across from a place where we keep them in the freezer and replace their blood with chemicals and fix them with putty and dress them up like dolls. That's not my future."

"But you're so good at it," Dad says.

"I'm good at a lot of stuff." I tick things off on my fingers. "Fixing computers, drawing, cooking—"

"People," Theo throws in. "You really understand people."

"Okay," I say, though I'm not sure I agree. "People, acting—"

Dee shakes her head. "You're a terrible actor."

I growl at her. "Whatever. The point is that being good at things doesn't mean I should spend the rest of my life doing them."

My mom is smiling at me. I've always suspected she might be persuaded to join my side, but in this moment, I don't know where she stands. "You're better than good at makeup. You're better than me."

"Then maybe I'll go to cosmetology school, or I'll study practical special effects for movies. Both of which are careers where I can work on the living instead of the dead."

Grandpa Karl and Grandma Jodi aren't heavily invested in my future as a mortician, so they sit and listen passively, but Grandma Sue tosses her napkin on the table. "You're sixteen—"

"Seventeen."

"You don't know what you want, young man." Her fierce eyes dare anyone to contradict her. "Your great-grandfather built DeLuca and Son's. He passed it to his son, who passed it to your father who will—"

"Pass it to his daughter," I say. "Delilah DeLuca. Who is amazing at what she does and actually loves it."

Red creeps across Dad's cheeks. "We'll discuss this at home, Dino."

I stand. "No, Dad, we won't. Because this isn't a discussion. This is me telling you and Mom and Grandma Sue, who doesn't even live with us but thinks she can tell me what to do with my life, that I have no idea what I'm going to be when I'm older, but I know what I'm not going to be. Deal with it."

And then I do the most July thing I can think of and walk away.

JULY

I RIDE UP FRONT INSTEAD OF IN THE TRUNK WHEN WE leave Loggerheads. Dino cracks the windows when we get going, but he doesn't mention the smell, which I'm grateful for.

"I can't believe I did it," he says. I don't know where we're going—I doubt Dino knows—but I'm happy for the moment to tag along for the ride. "You should have seen the looks on their faces. They were so surprised."

"No they weren't." When Dino glares at me, I say, "What?"

"Can't you let me have this?"

"Fine. Wow, I bet they were totally shocked to hear the thing they've suspected for years but refused to admit to avoid crushing their dreams of their son following in their footsteps. Good on you." I turn to him. "Better?"

"Why were we friends, again?"

"Because you were a freak and I was a freak, and being two

freaks together was better than being two freaks alone."

"You should put that on a T-shirt," Dino says.

"Maybe I will, but I doubt anyone would buy them."

Dino drives to the park near his house, grabs a blanket out of his trunk that I'd used for a pillow earlier, and we lie on the grass under the moonlit sky.

"Do you know how much dog shit there is in this grass?" I ask.

"That's why I brought the blanket."

"Right," I say. Then, "Hey, I'm sorry about your biology exam."

"Okay?"

I sit up on my elbow and look at Dino. "I'm serious. I should have stolen the money from Momma or beat up a Girl Scout. Screwing over your bio grade, even to take you to the greatest concert of your entire life, wasn't cool, and I'm sorry."

Dino's quiet for a moment. Then he says, "It *was* a great concert."

"Remember how the band came out wearing VR goggles?"

"Yeah. What was up with that?"

"I read that they'd rigged special cameras in the club to watch us in VR."

"So even though they were on stage, they were watching us in virtual reality instead of with their eyes?"

"Basically."

"That's really odd or really awesome."

"Why not both?"

Dino chuckles. "Wasn't that the night I got a flat tire on the way home and that Jeep full of Dr. Frank-N-Furters on their way to a *Rocky Horror Picture Show* party stopped to help us?"

"No, that was the night we told our parents we were going to Homecoming but went to that weird interactive play that was *Hamlet* in interpretive dance held in an old hotel."

"Yes!" Dino says. "I loved that play."

"I hated it."

"Only because they didn't let you talk while we explored."

I roll my eyes. "Fine. True." For this second, things feel the way they used to. Me and Dino against the world. We don't need anyone else, we don't want anyone else. We have each other, and that's enough.

"Dino?"

"Yeah?"

"I don't want to die," I say. "But I also kind of want to die."

"Yeah."

I slap his chest. "You're supposed to say you don't want me to die either."

"What if I do a little?" I slap him again and he laughs and says, "Kidding!"

"Seriously though, I keep thinking if I don't die, no one else will either. That woman in the hospital, countless others suffering throughout the world, your grandmother."

"Hey!"

"Do you honestly want her annoying you about not becoming a mortician for the rest of eternity?"

"On second thought," he says. "Go to the light, Grandma."

"So what do we do?"

"I don't know."

Dino's supposed to have the answer. I think I expected he'd solve this problem eventually. I get us into trouble; Dino gets us out. It's the way our relationship works best. Without me, he never would have gone to concerts or skipped school, and without him, I would have wound up in jail. But he doesn't have the answer this time. Maybe there isn't one.

"Why'd you actually break up with Rafi?" I ask. Mostly to fill the silence.

"I don't know that either."

"Do you like him?"

"Yeah."

"Are you romantically and sexually attracted to him?"

"Do we have to talk about this?"

I turn toward him. "We used to be able to talk about everything."

Dino sighs and then sits up and faces me. "Yes, I like him. He's funny and brave and compassionate. He's kind of conceited, too, but that's only to hide how massively insecure he is. He's handsome, and I think I'd be okay with him being my first but, truthfully, I'm not ready for anyone to be my first yet, not that he's pressured me. He's not like that." He pauses thoughtfully. "I think Rafi makes me a better person."

"Then why break up with him?"

"Maybe I don't want to be a better person," he says. "Maybe I liked me the way I was when I didn't care about how I dressed or when I cared more about sleeping in than I did about waking up before dawn to clean the beach."

I take Dino's hand and play with his fingers. "Remember how I said you'd changed?" Dino nods. "I meant it. But I don't think the changes are bad."

"Aren't they? I'm not me anymore, July."

"You'll always be you. This is simply a better version of you."

"But what if it's not who I want to be?"

I shrug. "Then you let it go. Become someone else for a while." I pause for a second. "But I don't think you broke up with Rafi because you disliked who you were becoming. I think you did it because you were afraid you didn't deserve to become that person."

"No," Dino says. "That's not—"

"Sure it is. But Rafi was right. You deserve to be loved. You deserve to become whoever you want to be."

"That's not it!" Dino says, cutting me off.

"What is it, then?"

Dino hangs his head. "The more I changed, the more I spent time with Rafi and the kids from the center, the further I got from you. I got Rafi, but I lost you."

I don't know what to say.

"I think that's why I was so angry," he goes on. "I was mad at me for changing, and I was mad at you for being mad at me for changing, especially since I wasn't even certain I liked the person I was turning into. There I was, play-testing Dino 2.0, and I needed to know I could scoot a little closer to the edge and that you'd catch me if I lost my balance. But you left me, and I hated you for that."

I keep moving my lips, but no words come out. When I don't speak for a full minute, Dino turns from me. I don't know what to say or what he expects me to say. I don't know how to respond to what he told me. So I do the only thing that makes sense.

"Come on," I say. "We have to go."

"Where?" Dino asks. His voice sounds so exhausted, and I'm starting to feel tired too.

"Rafi's. You need to tell him what you told me."

DINO

RAFI'S CAR IS IN THE DRIVEWAY AND THE LIGHTS IN THE house are on. His parents' cars are also in the driveway, so there's no way I'm knocking on the door and dealing with them.

"What does it matter if I tell him?" I say. "Let's leave."

I move to turn the engine on, but July plucks the keys from the ignition. "You obviously like the guy," she says. "Even if you don't know if you love him yet. You're an idiot for breaking up with him. Tell him what you told me, and let *him* decide. He put up with your shit for the last year. He deserves the chance to make up his own mind."

"Fine." I get out my phone to text him that I'm outside. He doesn't reply, but I decide to give him ten minutes before bailing. "Oh," I say. "I found something for you." I text a link to July. "You should take a look at it."

"What is it?"

"Maybe a way for you to talk to your parents and to Jo."

July looks at me, intrigued. "How—"

She's interrupted by a knock on the car window. Rafi's standing there looking handsome, but a little rougher around then edges than usual.

"Go," July says. "And be honest."

I get out of the car and shut it behind me.

"Hey," Rafi says. He's wearing a pair of black running shorts and a white tank top, and he looks like he's either on his way to the gym or getting home from it.

"Sorry to drop by—"

"No! I'm glad you did."

"Yeah?"

"Not that I've been sitting at home eating peanut butter Oreos and watching horror movies."

"Horror movies?"

He nods. "Some people deal with breakups by watching sappy movies and crying it out; I deal by watching crappy horror movies and rooting for the killers."

I stuff my hands in my pockets. "Maybe we should talk over here in front of your house. Where it's well lit."

Rafi smiles. His face is a symphony; his dimples, lips, and beautiful amber eyes performing one perfect movement. "I've missed you, Dino."

"You saw me yesterday."

"I've missed the idea of you."

Being July was a hell of a lot easier when it was me against my parents. I'd seen July stand up to adults more times than I could count. Even when she didn't know who she was, she fought for the right to screw up and figure it out on her own. But I'd never seen July do this. I'd never seen her uncertain or confused. Not in a meaningful way.

"Did you break up with me because I'm trans?" Rafi asks.

"What? No! Definitely not."

Rafi breathes a sigh of relief, and I hate that it was a question he felt like he needed to ask, but I can't be upset with him for asking.

"This is difficult for me," I say. I feel exposed out here, standing on the sidewalk with July in the car pretending not to listen, and Rafi's parents at the window inside pretending not to watch.

"More difficult than breaking up with me?"

I nod.

"Then just say it, Dino." A note of frustration's crept into his voice. "You can't hurt me more than you already have."

That last bit stings, but I deserve it. "I like you, Rafi. A lot."

"I like you too. More than like."

Rafi tries to take my hand, but I pull away. I'm afraid if he touches me I'll melt and won't get through the things I need to say.

"For this huge chunk of my life, I had July, and I didn't need anyone else. She accepted me for who I was and never asked me to change. I could be lazy and indecisive and cynical and ambivalent about the world. July and I were these binary stars endlessly orbiting each other, and that made me happy.

"Then you came along."

Rafi doesn't speak, but tears fill the rims of his eyes, and I'll lose it if he cries.

"You came along and you changed me."

"I didn't mean to," Rafi says. "I wasn't trying to."

"It's okay," I tell him. "I needed to change." I can't resist anymore, so I reach out and take his hand. It's moist and trembling, but I keep holding it and hope we can get through this.

"You challenged me, Rafi. I started to care about things I never cared about before. You showed me this whole world I didn't know existed; this community I could be a part of."

"You're still a part of it," he says. "Even if we're not together anymore."

I can't help laughing. "See? This is who you are. I broke up with you, and you're still looking after me. You're amazing and wonderful and—"

"A total wreck." Rafi wipes his nose with his free hand. "I'm not perfect. I'm insecure and moody and—"

"I know." I wish I didn't have to cut him off—it's kind of nice hearing Rafi list his deficiencies—but I need to finish what I started or I never will. "My point is that I began to change, and July and I drifted away from each other, which made me uncertain I should change, resent you for making me want to change, and hate her for not giving me the space to see who I might become *and* for not being there for me if I decided to come back."

Rafi inches closer, moving inside my defenses. "And then she died."

"Yeah." I look into his eyes and stumble. Everything I've said up to now was the easy part. Now for the hard part. "I broke up with you because I don't know who I am. More than that, I don't know who I want to be. I don't know if I belong in the community you're part of. Sometimes I feel like I do, other times I feel like I'm as much of an outsider as I've ever been. But that was okay when July was alive because there was always some part of me that believed if I got lost and needed to come home, she'd be there to guide me. But she won't. She can't. She's gone, and I'm terrified that I'll stay with you and become this whole other person and look up one day and not like who I am."

Confusion haunts Rafi's eyes and mouth. His lips move, but it's clear he doesn't know what to say.

"When you told me you loved me, I knew you were all in. But I'm not. Not yet. I'm not ready to leave behind who I was with July."

"Dino," he says. "No. I don't want you to. You think I love you because you go with me to charity runs and to scare off those annoying tourists who bother nesting turtles?"

"Kind of, yeah."

Rafi shakes his head. "You think I want you to change?"

"No, but—"

"No buts," he says. "I fell for the guy I met at the Apple store who spent ten minutes interrogating Siri about her plans to subjugate humanity. The guy who made me watch every episode of *Black Mirror* on our second date so I'd, in his words, *really understand you*. The guy who thinks it's plausible that the government is slowly changing the words in e-books in order to brainwash the populace."

"It's totally possible!"

"And you've changed me, too," he says. "The first Saturday of the summer, I picked you up to drive to Palm Beach to protest the president and you convinced me to skip it and go to Disney instead."

"Which was fun, admit it."

Rafi holds up his hand. "It was one of my most favorite days, but it's not an idea I would have come up with on my own." He shrugs. "I don't want to date me, Dino. I want to date you."

"But I don't know who I am."

"Then figure it out," he says.

"And if you don't like the end result?"

"Then I dump you. Obviously." He coughs and says, "Not that I'm assuming we're getting back together. It was a hypothetical. Unless you want to."

There's hope in his eyes. In the way his hand tenses around mine and in the way his shoulders sit a little higher.

"I don't know what to do," I say. "You said you love me, and I can't say it back because I want to say it and mean it, and I'm not there yet."

"I understand."

"Do you?" I ask. "Because you deserve someone great, and I'm not certain I'm that person. I want to be—I hope I can be—but I might not be him. We might go out again and I'll realize in a month that we're better apart. Or you might realize you don't like who I'm becoming or—"

"I get it."

"I don't want to hurt you."

Rafi smiles. "I don't want you to hurt me either, but so long as you don't do it on purpose, I won't have to kill you."

"Please be sure," I say. "I really want to kiss you, but I won't if you're not sure."

"Dino, I'm sure."

JULY

OH, GROSS. HOW LONG ARE THEY GOING TO BE OUT there choking on each other's tongues? I don't think I can watch much more of this. It was painful enough listening to Dino spend twenty minutes fumbling with what he was trying to say. The boy takes a million words to say what could've been said with, "I'm a moron; please forgive me." Now I've got to watch them slobber all over each other. I'm pretty sure *this* is the bad place.

Whatever. I roll up the window since they're clearly done talking and pull out the message Dino sent me before he took off to spill his feelings for Rafi on the sidewalk, then I click the link.

"What the?"

It's for a service called the Past. People write e-mails or letters that are kept in the Past and then, if they die, their pre-selected "executor" notifies the Past, and the letters or e-mails are sent to the intended recipients. I may be not-dead, but I'm dead-dead as far as my folks and Jo are concerned, which means I can't talk to them and tell them the things I wish I'd said when I was alive. But with this, I can. I can tell Momma how I know we fought constantly, but that she was the one who taught me to fight, and I'm glad she did. I can tell Daddy that I'm sorry I didn't spend more time with him after the divorce but that I was angry with him when I shouldn't have been. And I can tell Jo . . . well, I can tell her everything she'll need to know to be a badass. Or rather, how to be a better badass than me.

Dino gets into the car and watches Rafi practically dance into his house.

"You're glowing," I say. "Stop it."

"We're back together."

"I figured by the disgusting make-up make out I witnessed."

Dino has the decency to blush. "Sorry."

I turn to him fiercely. "Don't ever apologize for being happy, Dino. Not to me. Not to anyone." I settle down and then turn my phone toward him. "So what the hell's the deal with this?"

Dino clears his throat. "Oh. That. I thought you could send letters to Jo or your mom or whoever."

"Yeah, I can read the promotional copy on the website," I say. "But do you think it's fair?"

"To whom?"

"To my mom or Jo or whoever?" I stare at the website, which features a happy family leering at a tablet, reading a letter that's probably from dear old dead Grandpa Lester who stayed with them during the holidays, clogged every toilet in the house, and horrified them with stories that frequently began with "I'm not racist, but . . ."

"I don't know," I say. "This feels like I'd be opening the wound again."

"Or," Dino says, "letters from you might be the salve that allows them to heal, or helps them heal a little faster."

He has a point, though I'm not going to admit it to him. Still, I need some time to think it through.

"Home?" Dino asks. "Or rather, the funeral home, since my grandparents have invaded my bedroom and my life and I doubt I'll get a single hot shower until they're gone?"

"Actually," I say, "can we go to Truman?"

"The high school?"

"I kind of want to peek in on rehearsals."

Dino looks at the time on the stereo clock. It's a little after eight. "You think they'll still be there?"

"Opening night is next week, and they recently replaced their lead. They'll be there."

He hesitates but finally nods. "Fine." Dino winds through Rafi's neighborhood, heading toward Truman High.

"Did you mean what you said to Rafi?" I ask while we drive.

"Which part?"

"About hating me for not giving you the space to explore who you were?" I bite my lip and glance at him side-eye. "Is that the real reason you stayed so pissed at me?"

Dino lets out a long sigh. "Kind of. There were a lot of reasons. I wanted you to meet Rafi and his friends, but I also didn't.

I was mad at you for having plans anytime I invited you to hang out, but I was also happy, because I got to keep my worlds separate. I didn't want Rafi to judge me for who I was when I was with you, or for you to judge me for who I was when I was with Rafi. I hated that you made jokes about Rafi and my friends, but I also wanted to be making those jokes with you."

"Were you embarrassed by me?" I ask. "Were you afraid they'd like me better?"

Dino shakes his head. "I'm used to people liking you better. It's just, you were mine and I wanted to keep you to myself."

I'm trying to wrap my brain around it. "So you wanted me to want to spend time with you and Rafi, but you didn't want me to actually *want* to spend time with y'all?"

"Pretty much."

"You are so damned confusing."

"I learned from the best." Dino flashes me a smile. It's genuine and real, and I hope he smiles like that for the rest of his life and never stops.

"You and Rafi are cute together," I say. "Don't screw it up."

"I'll try." His smile softens slightly. "I wish I felt about him the way he feels about me, you know? If I could wake up tomorrow and be in love with him, I'd do it."

I roll my eyes at Dino. "That's not how love works."

"Oh yeah? How does it work, then?"

"Love isn't obvious until you're in it," I say. "It's not a punch in the face that leaves you reeling. Love is gradual and sneaky. It grows like weeds between the cracks of a hundred average moments."

Dino's quiet for a minute. We drive in silence and I think I've said something to upset him, but when I rewind the conversation in my mind, I can't see where I might've gone wrong. But then he turns to me when we stop at a red light and he grabs me and wraps his arms around me and hugs me until the light turns green.

DINO

JULY DIRECTS ME TO THE PARKING LOT BEHIND THE
theater, which is way nicer than the one at Palm Shores High.
There are only two vehicles parked there—a truck and a Honda.

"You sure they're still here?"

"Trust me," July says. Not that she's giving me much choice.
I follow her in through the rear door, which is propped open
with a brick, and we walk quietly through the maze of curtains
and lights. Before I see Zora, I hear her. Her husky voice fills the
theater like thunder, backed by a recording of the band. There's
a careful carelessness to the way she sings that makes me feel
like she could smash into the wall at any moment and burst into
flames. That she doesn't is a testament to her skill.

"Damn," I whisper, "she's really good."

July purses her lips and then punches me in the arm.

We peek around the curtain. Zora's standing center stage in a dress that's saggy in the bust and loose in the waist, belting out "Good Morning Baltimore."

"I didn't need any padding to fill out the dress," July says with pride.

"Not everyone can have your curves."

We've only been here a minute, but I'm already nervous that we're going to get caught. I don't know why July wanted to come. Seeing Zora Hood rehearsing for the role July has wanted to play since she first heard Tracy Turnblad sing must be torture. It might not be so terrible if Zora couldn't carry a tune, but she sings with a confidence and dexterity that are admirable. I wouldn't say Zora's better than July, mostly because July would shove my testicles into my nostrils, but she's pretty damn good.

"Come on." I tug July's sleeve as the song comes to an end, but she doesn't move.

Zora holds onto the last note and then nails the finish. The music ends.

"Motherfucker!" Zora says. "Mr. Moore was an imbecile for making me July's understudy."

I pull July more urgently. As much as July may want to watch Zora unfairly castigate herself for a performance that was objectively good, I don't. Only, July doesn't budge. In fact, she pulls her arm out of my grasp and marches onto the stage.

"Yeah he was," July says in a loud, clear voice. "You should've gotten the lead and *I* should've been the understudy."

Not unexpectedly, Zora screams.

JULY

ZORA TAKES THE TRUTH SURPRISINGLY WELL. DINO AND I had to hide in the dressing room and then sneak out to the car after Zora's screams brought Mr. Moore, who'd been sleeping in the office, running onto the stage. She told him a palmetto bug had crawled across her foot, and he'd bought the story but decided it was time to close up, so we wound up standing around Dino's car in the lot. It's not much of a step up from the Taco Bell lot, but at least there are no cops here.

Dino and I switch off trying to explain the events of the past couple of days to her, though it's not like our grasp on the situation is particularly firm, and when we're done, Zora kind of smiles and nods.

"I knew you were real!"

"Yeah," I say. "Sorry about that. I panicked and Dino played along."

"Totally understandable. If I rose from the grave and got caught joyriding in my best friend's car, I'd have done the same." Zora's sitting on the hood of Dino's car with her hands in her lap. "Or not. No, I probably would've led you on a high-speed chase, blown a tire, and died in a fiery explosion." She pauses. "Is it weird being a zombie?"

"Not a zombie," I say.

"If you say so."

Dino keeps eyeing Zora like he expects this is a trap somehow. "You can't tell anyone. Please promise you won't tell a single person."

"Why not?" Zora says. "You could start a video channel. Zombie makeup tips. Do you know how many people would watch that?"

It's scary that I think a lot of people would watch, but that's not the point. "Zora, promise you won't tell anyone."

Zora sighs like we're morons for not seeing the genius of her plan. "Fine."

"Thank you," Dino says.

"Are you going to stay this way forever? Because if you need a place to crash, my brother's at college and my parents are oblivious."

"I don't know," I say. "I really, really hope this isn't permanent. The smell is getting worse."

Zora grins and taps her nose. "Doesn't bother me. I took a softball to the skull in fourth grade. Since then, everything smells like Jolly Ranchers." She leans in and takes a whiff. "Mmmmm. Watermelon."

Dino gags. "And on that horrifying note, we should get going." He jingles his keys in the air.

Zora slides off the car. "Hey, I know you said no one else can know—"

I'm already shaking my head. Even though I'm not sure where she's going with this, I know it's somewhere terrible.

"Hear me out," Zora says. "It's my mom's boss. Think you could pretend to be a zombie? He keeps harassing her, and a good scare from you might convince him to keep his grabby hands off her ass."

"No way," Dino starts, but I'm like, "Now, that's not a bad idea."

"Yes it is," Dino says.

I flash Dino an eye roll. "How about this, Zora. If I'm still not-dead in a week, we'll talk."

"Deal." Zora climbs into her truck and takes off.

Dino's giving me an ugly face, which, to be fair, could be one of the many in his repertoire. But this one's vastly uglier than the rest. "Are you seriously going to play zombie for Zora?"

"Maybe," I say. "If I end up stuck like this forever, I'll have to find a way to have some fun."

Dino and I get in the car. As he starts the engine, he mutters, "We have got to find a way to rekill you."

DINO

THE UNIVERSE HAS SHIFTED. I FEEL IT THE WAY SOME dogs can sense earthquakes or seizures. The change is minute, but recognizable. And I don't know what it means.

"Can we go to the beach?" July asks, and I don't answer, but I take the next U-turn and make my way there.

July's never met a silence she didn't want to fill, but since we left Truman High she's been pretty quiet, and I might have imagined it, but I think I saw her yawn.

I park on the side of the road, and we walk down to the water.

"You know?" I say, "I really hate the beach."

July barks out a laugh. "Tell me more, Florida boy."

"Seriously. The water smells like you half the time, seaweed is disgusting, sea lice are even worse."

"You ever gotten them . . ." July motions at my crotch.

"More often than I want to think about. And it itches so much worse than you think." Dino shrugs. "Then there's the sand. It's a giant human litter box. You wouldn't believe the crap, literal and figurative, people bury in the sand."

July mumbles something, and when I ask what, she says, "I guess you and your boyfriend see a lot of that down here cleaning the place up."

She says "your boyfriend" with a bit of an edge that confuses me. "What's going on?" I ask. "Are you pissed that I made up with Rafi?"

"No," she says. "And yes."

I throw up my hands. "What the hell, July? You're the one who told me to do it. You're the one who forced me to drive to his house and be honest with him."

"Like I had to put a gun to your head," she says. Her words are bitter and her tone biting, but I get the impression they're a smoke screen to hide what she's actually feeling.

"Are you going to take Rafi to the wedding tomorrow?" July asks, making it clear she's not interested in finishing our previous conversation.

"He already has the suit."

July lets out a sigh, but it doesn't sound like a sigh. Instead it sounds like someone blowing across the top of an open bottle, dry and dusty. "Look, when you have sex with him, it better be your choice. Don't let him make you feel guilty for wanting to wait or tell you that you owe it to him or any of that stupid shit guys say."

Now I'm really confused. "What the hell are you talking about? Sex is the furthest thing from my mind."

"Liar."

"I'm not lying, but I am becoming annoyed."

July turns from me and covers her mouth with her hand.

"There!" I shout. "What was that? What are you doing?"

"I yawned, Dino," she says. "Alert the media."

"But you don't need to yawn due to your lack of a functioning set of lungs. And it's not like you sleep, either. So what was that?"

July stops walking and I stop walking, and she looks out across the ocean, but I'm looking at her when she says, "The end. I think."

"The end?"

"Yes. And I'm trying to tell you what you need to know so that you don't screw up the rest of your life."

"But what do you know about sex?"

"More than you."

"That bored hand job you gave Kris Waterson on the bus to Universal Studios in eighth grade makes you an expert?"

She shakes her head. Glances up at me with iron in her eyes. "You're not the July Cooper expert you think you are. A lot can happen in a year."

"Did you do it with someone? Who was it? When? Why didn't you tell me?"

"Because you weren't around!" she shouts. "You weren't there before to talk me out of it, you weren't there after to listen to me talk about it, and you weren't there for the horrifying three days I thought I was pregnant to help me get through it!" Her voice softens. "You weren't there."

"I'm here now." I take her hand.

"And how much good does that do me seeing as I'm dead?" She pulls her hand away and starts walking again.

I lag behind, unsure if I want to chase her or if she wants me to catch up to her. But it's not like I can abandon her out here.

"I do think about sex," I say. "With Rafi. Sometimes."

"Obviously," July mutters.

"Not as much as you think. But the idea of it makes me nervous."

"The special considerations that might be involved with sleeping with Rafi?"

"No, though I've thought about that too," I say. "I'm freaked by the abstract idea of sex." July glances at me, her mouth a frown, her eyebrows dipping down. "I'm not worried about what goes where and who sticks it there."

"That sounds like the worst picture book ever," she says. "Or the best."

I throw her an "I'm trying to be serious here" look, and she mimes zipping her lips shut, which I figure buys me approximately thirty seconds of silence. "Like I said, I'm not sweating the details because I figure that if I do it with Rafi, far in the future, he's the kind of guy who'll want to take it slow and talk about it so that we're both confident and comfortable about everything that happens."

"What's the abstract terror, then?" July asks.

"It's what sex means." I struggle to find the words. "Doing it with Rafi, or any guy, means accepting this label that people will use to judge me for the rest of my life. They'll use it to make assumptions about me, and then act like I'm a weirdo when I don't fit into the box they keep trying to stuff me into."

July nudges me. "Sex doesn't determine who you are."

"But it determines who other people think I am," I say. "Sometimes I wish we didn't have to deal with this nonsense. Why should anyone have to come out? Why should anyone have to reveal their sexual identity?"

"Convenience?" July says. "If we don't know whether someone is gay or straight or bi or asexual, how can we know whether or not they might be interested in us?"

"Walk up and ask them," I say. When July laughs, I keep going. "I'm serious. Why should it be such a big deal for me to walk up to a guy I think is cute at Starbucks or the bookstore or wherever and ask him out?"

"What if he's not interested?"

"Then he says, 'No thank you.' Why is that so difficult? If I ask a guy out, it's not because I think he's into guys, it's because I think he's cute and hope he's into *me*."

"I don't think we're evolved enough to live in that world yet, Dino."

"No, I guess we're not."

July tries to stifle another yawn, this one bigger than before. She catches me watching her and turns away. "Stop staring."

"Do you think—"

"It was Manny," July says.

"What was Manny?"

Her eyes dart up at me. "The guy I did it with."

I grab her wrist and pull her to a stop. "Wait. You said that rumor wasn't true."

July shakes her head. "I said I didn't start it."

This is kind of blowing my mind. "I have so many questions."

"And I'm not going to answer them," she says. "But I will tell you that it happened at a party, it lasted from 1:04 a.m. until 1:11 a.m., and I have not stopped regretting it since."

I move in to hug July, but she pushes me away. "What?"

"I needed you then," she says. "I don't need you now."

"Why are you being like this?" I ask. "Yawning and treating me like I'm not your best friend?"

July says, "You were right. We're the reason I rose from the dead, but not so we could finish fighting about our friendship. So we could let go of it. I'm yawning because one of us has." As if to punctuate her statement, another yawn ripples through her, and she doesn't try to hide it.

"Me?"

"Just like before. You have Rafi now; you don't need me."

"What the hell, July? Friendship isn't a zero-sum game! Can't I love you both? Can't I have you both in my life?"

"No."

"Why not?"

"I'm dead, Dino. Let me die."

My whole body is shaking, but I don't know it's from anger or fear, or who I'm angry at or what I'm afraid of. "What does that even mean?"

July shoves me. "It means leave."

"Stop it."

She shoves me again. This time so hard I fall on my ass in the sand. "Go home, Dino."

I scramble to my feet. "And then what? You die out here? Some tourist finds your corpse?"

"Let me worry about that," she says. "But I don't want you around anymore."

"I get it," I say. "I'm like the dog or the alien or whatever that you have to threaten to get it to return to where it belongs. You gonna throw a rock at me next?"

"If I have to."

"Fine, you want me to go? I'm gone. But don't come crawling back from the dead when you realize you miss me this time."

"Don't worry," July says. "I won't."

JULY

I TOSS THE CONTROLLER ON THE FLOOR AND DANCE around the room chanting, "You're dead! You're dead," because while I'm definitely a shitty loser, I'm an even worse winner.

"How do I keep getting my ass handed to me by zombie Barbie?" Zora Hood says.

"Not a zombie."

When I told Dino to leave, I hadn't actually thought through what was happening or what I was going to do. I kind of figured he'd take off and I'd get more tired and roll myself into the ocean so sharks could eat me. Or something. It's not like my parents would ever discover I wasn't in my coffin in the cemetery. Only, while the yawns kept coming, I didn't feel an overwhelming urge to sleep. Seeing as I'd gotten rid of Dino in such dramatic fashion, I didn't want to ruin it by begging him for a ride. So I called the only other person who knew I was not-dead.

Yeah. I *am* regretting that decision.

Zora's room is kind of disgusting. We were friendly, but we weren't friends, and I'd never been to her house. She lives in a duplex near the railroad tracks in the kind of neighborhood my mom would lock the doors while driving through, which would definitely be making presumptuous and erroneous assumptions about the people who live here. The house itself is fine; it's Zora's bedroom that's gross. When the girl who's literally rotting from the inside out is afraid of catching the plague or a flesh-eating bacterial infection, you might want to do a little spring cleaning.

"We've been in theater together for two years," I say. "How did I not know you gamed?"

Zora stretches her legs out in front of her. "You never asked."

The answer is technically true, and it hits like a slap. "Was I that self-absorbed?"

"Kind of." Zora's head bobs on her shoulders. It's not quite a nod, but it's close. "Don't get upset about it. We're all a little self-absorbed."

"Some of us more than others, apparently."

"Sure but . . ." Zora stops whatever she was going to say and seemingly changes course. "I liked you, July. I admired you. But I was happy when I heard you'd died because I thought I'd finally gotten my shot. I thought I was going to have to wait for you to graduate before escaping your shadow. Don't get me wrong, I was obviously sad you'd died, but your death shoved me to the front of the line a year early."

Zora dumps it out there without the slightest trace of

self-recrimination or embarrassment, and I don't know how to respond. "Glad I could help?"

"Whatever," she says. "Point is, we're basically selfish animals. I wish we could've been friends when you weren't a zombie, but I'm glad for the chance to get to know you now."

"Me too. I think." I fake a cough so that I can change the subject. "You don't have to entertain me. Sleep, eat, do whatever weird activities you do when there's not an animated corpse hiding in your room."

Zora glances at the TV and then the controllers. "This *is* what I do. Aside from rehearsing for the musical. And working."

"You have a job?"

"McDonalds." Zora wrinkles her nose. "My parents need whatever help they can get, and I don't mind." She shrugs. "Most nights I'm awake until three or four in the morning, and then I sleep until noon."

"Great." I'd eat some brains for ten minutes of quiet. Since I won't be getting that, I pick up the controller and convince Zora to play a couple more games, and I even let her win one. Probably because I'm preoccupied thinking about Dino and how I keep yawning but I'm not getting any more tired, so I don't know what to do. Zora heads out into the kitchen for a few minutes and comes back with a plate of little bagel pizzas.

"Do you have to eat those in front of me?" I snap.

Zora, sitting in her desk chair, spins around so that she's not facing me anymore.

"Ha-ha."

"Do you want one?" She holds one of the bagel pizzas in the air.

"How many times do I have to tell you that I can't eat?"

Zora rotates to face me. "I'm not holding you hostage. You can leave whenever you want." She says it with a smile that's equal parts sweet and creepy.

"Seriously, I used to think you were a shy loser who spent her nights scheming ways to shove me off the stage so I'd break my leg and you could steal my place, but that you lacked the spine to actually do it."

"Ouch."

"I'm glad I underestimated you."

"Is that an apology?"

"Call it whatever you want," I say. "It's just that I'm frustrated as hell." I run my hand through my hair. It's starting to feel a little brittle, and I look at my fingers to make certain it's not coming out in clumps. "I didn't ask to die, but it happened. Don't I deserve my white light and a heaven full of puppies that never grow up into annoying dogs and stores that only serve free cake? Instead, I get this. A not-death tied to a rotting body where I can't see my family and the only friend I have pretty much hates me."

Zora clears her throat. "Plus, you're most likely responsible for the pain and suffering of the people who can't die but wish they could."

"I don't know what else to do!" I say. "I let my family bury me and have their closure. I fixed Dino and his stupid hot boyfriend so that he could let me go, and then I kicked his ass so he'd leave. What am I missing?"

Zora sets the plate of bagel pizzas on her desk and sits on the floor beside me. A second later, she scoots a bit farther away. "You ever think this isn't about them? That it might be about you?"

"Only every second since I woke up. But, as Dino keeps saying, not everything's about me."

"Right," Zora says. "Well, what if this is?"

"Explain."

"Maybe your parents and your sister and Dino aren't the ones who need to let go. Maybe you are."

"Oh, I let go."

Zora wrinkles her nose in this way she has that kind of makes her look like a cute piglet. "Have you? Because I get the impression that you never let go of anything."

I tap my fingers on my legs to keep my hands busy so I don't strangle her.

"Listen," Zora says. "I'm not saying this situation isn't weird, but it does kind of make sense. You had Dino and you never made much of an attempt to be friendly with anyone else."

"I was friendly!"

"When you wanted something." She pauses and waits for me to argue, but I can't, seeing as our friendship began when I called her and asked her for help. "You may have had other friends, but he was your anchor. Even Mrs. Larsen mentioned how much you'd changed after Dino dropped out of theater."

"Teachers were gossiping about me?"

Zora shrugs. "One teacher."

I think about what Zora said, and maybe she's right. I was so certain Dino was the one clinging to our friendship that I didn't stop to think that it might be me.

"I recognize that face," Zora says. "You have an idea. Do tell."

It's not much of a plan, and I doubt it will work, but it's what I've got. "Do you have a dress I can fit into?"

Zora grabs my hand and pulls me to my feet. "Let's find out."

DINO

I'M DREAMING ABOUT RAFI. JULY PROBABLY THINKS MY Rafi dreams are naked romps through fields of cake, but they're actually pretty mundane. We go to the mall and hold hands and shop for books or a new case for my phone or socks. We go to the movies and argue over the snacks—he insists on dumping M&Ms into the popcorn, and I think it's sacrilege to ruin hot, buttery popcorn in such a grotesque fashion—but then we spend the movie trying to pretend we're not intentionally letting our greasy fingers linger together in the bucket.

And then someone I'm going to kill is shaking me awake. Delilah is standing over me looking like she's murdered someone and needs my help dismembering the body, which is silly since she could butcher a corpse far more efficiently than me, and she's opening her mouth and spitting out words, but I don't understand them because I'm still hearing Rafi's voice telling me he loves me.

Reality needs load screens, like in video games. Gentle transition animations to ease us from one state to the next so that waking into reality doesn't completely jar our fragile brains. We're meant to enjoy dreams, but how can we when the return to consciousness sucks so hard?

I try to sit up and pull the blankets over me and crunch myself into as small a ball as possible.

"Jesus, Dee, what time is it?"

"Four something," she says. "But didn't you hear me? I'm calling off the wedding." Delilah's wearing a long T-shirt that I assume once belonged to Theo, and she's pacing back and forth in front of the couch I was trying to sleep on, spewing nonsense into the air like ash from an erupting volcano.

"You're not calling off the wedding."

"Of course I am! Everyone should call their weddings off. Weddings are an outdated tool of the patriarchy. Before you know it I'm going to be popping out babies and I'll have to quit my job to stay home with them and they'll consume my identity. I'll stop being Delilah DeLuca, kick-ass mortician to the rich and famous, and I'll become Delilah Kang, soccer mom."

Even if I'd had the chance to ease from my dreams into this nightmare, it's still a lot. Delilah's shorting out my ability to think. "First off," I say, "where are all these rich and famous dead people you've been working on?"

"Do you think I'm joking, Dino?"

Delilah doesn't do overwrought. She's calm, methodical. Even at her most bridezilla, she was merely slightly pushy. When she was in her third year of college, she took on too many classes but didn't realize it until the middle of the semester. Instead of freaking out and flunking or buying drugs to help get her through the coursework, she calmly spoke to one of her professors, explained the situation, and worked out a deal to allow her to take an incomplete and finish the assignments the next semester. That's who she is. Queen *and* King of Calm.

"Are you pregnant?" I ask.

"No," she says. "Not yet."

I shake my head. "Then don't get pregnant until you're ready. There's a birth control procedure Theo can have done that's totally reversible, you're on the pill, and you can keep using condoms if you want to be extra cautious."

Delilah stops pacing. "How the hell do you know that?"

"Sex ed at Palm Shores is super comprehensive."

"Whatever," Dee says. "Theo still wants to have kids eventually. So do I, I guess."

"You guess?"

Delilah flops down on the couch beside me. "No, I do. But I've already seen some of my friends from school travel this path and it's like they transform from interesting people with lives who do things into people who have babies and talk about babies and post pictures of babies on every social media site they have a log-in for. All the hopes and dreams they had for their careers and lives get funneled into their babies."

"Why do you think you'd ever be one of those people?"

"Because why wouldn't I be?"

"Our mom, for one," I say. "She didn't trade in her combat boots for whatever kind of sensible shoes the stereotypical Stepford moms wear in your prewedding fever dreams. She didn't quit her job. She didn't give up anything." I shrug. "The baby-picture-posting fixation I can't help you with. I'm pretty certain babies emit brain altering chemicals that instigate that behavior and make it impossible to resist. Sorry."

Delilah bows her head and pulls her legs under her. "I'm not Mom, though."

I eye the tattoos on her arms and the way her hair, while not the same color, is cut almost identical to our mom's. I briefly consider pointing those details out to her, but I doubt she's in the mood to appreciate them.

"You're right," I say. "You're Delilah DeLuca: Kicker of Asses, Taker of Names, Waker of Brothers Who Haven't Gotten Decent Sleep in Three Days."

Before I can stop her, Delilah wraps me in a hug and squeezes until I can barely breathe. "Thanks, Dino."

"Does this count as my wedding gift to you?"

She squeezes a little harder and whispers, "No. I really want the knife set I registered for."

Finally, she lets go and sinks into the couch. "So, you doing okay? You've been gone a lot. Trying to avoid the grandparents?"

Now that July's funeral is done, the questions feel less intrusive. My parents are still dodging the topic of July's death, but funerals are basically the demarcation line for most people, after which the bereaved are expected to put it behind them and move on with their lives. Not that grief actually works that way.

"Broke up with Rafi—"

"Oh, Dino, I'm so sorry."

"Got back together with Rafi."

"Then I'm not sorry."

I can't exactly tell Delilah the rest—that I've been running around town with the animated corpse of my ex–best friend, trying to figure out how to get her to stay dead—so I say, "Pretty messed up about how people have stopped dying, huh?"

Delilah frowns like she knows exactly what I'm doing by bringing this up. "Maybe."

"Maybe?" I say. "So you don't think the suspension of death throughout the world is cause for alarm? You don't think that if this keeps up, not only will you and Mom and Dad be out of a job, but that the population explosion will quickly overwhelm the world?"

"Sure," she says. "All of that, yeah. But it's not permanent."

"And you know that how?"

"People die. It's the order of things." She shrugs. "It'll crank up again."

"Okay, but now I think it's weird how calm you are."

"I've had my freak out for the year," she says. "Besides, it's kind of nice."

I look at her like her head's been replaced by a lobster. My thoughts drift to the woman in the emergency room missing part of her head and that guy who wanted to die. "How is it nice?"

Dee pats my arm. "Because it reminds us what death actually is."

"Permanent?"

"Necessary."

DINO

I HAVE NO IDEA HOW TO TIE A BOW TIE. I STAND IN FRONT of the mirror and twist it into a knot that looks like a toddler did it.

"Do you know how to tie a bow tie?" I ask.

Rafi's lounging on my bed in a black-and-blue checkered suit that looks phenomenal on him. Honestly, I may as well wear a bathrobe to the wedding. No one's going to be looking at me with him by my side.

"Sorry. Bow ties aren't one of my many skills."

"Damn." I strip the tie off to try again. "Oh, sorry about earlier. I should've mentioned that my grandma can get a little handsy."

Rafi smiles, and God what a smile it is. "I'm used to it. I volunteered at a nursing home for a while. And it's not like she felt me up. Anyway, you're just not a touchy kind of guy."

"I like it when you touch me."

"Is that so?" Rafi stands and moves toward me, but then stops and clears his throat. "Hey, Mr. DeLuca."

My dad's standing in the doorway and I'm a little embarrassed, wondering how much of that he heard, but then I also don't care. If he didn't want to hear me flirting with my boyfriend, he shouldn't have been eavesdropping.

"You look nice, Rafi."

"Thank you, sir."

Dad doesn't say it, but I get the feeling he's trying to indicate that he wants to talk to me alone. Thankfully, Rafi also notices. "I think I'll go see if there are any of those waffles left."

As soon as Rafi leaves, Dad walks into the room and takes his place standing beside me. "Problem with the tie?"

"Yeah," I say. "The problem is that it's not a clip-on."

Dad moves behind me and arranges the tie around my neck so that the wide end hangs lower than the narrow. "Didn't I teach you how to do this?"

"I can tie a regular tie, but this thing is the devil's handiwork."

Dad laughs and then slowly walks me through the steps. "It's not as difficult as you think."

I try to follow what he's doing, but I get lost when he folds the left side and pulls the right side up through the neck. When he finishes, he tugs the ends to tighten it, looks at me appraisingly, and smiles.

"What?"

Dad shrugs and rests his hands on my shoulders. "You never

let me show you how to do stuff like this. You taught yourself to shave from YouTube videos, your mom taught you how to change a tire and the oil in your car, and I don't think anyone had to teach you how to make up decedents. You were born with that talent."

I pull away from him. "Not today, Dad, okay?"

"I'm not here to lecture you."

"Then, what?"

"You have a gift, son—"

"Please," I say. "Stop right there. Whatever you're about to tell me about how I have a gift and it's my responsibility to use it, blah, blah, blah. I don't want to hear it. I also have a life. It's mine, and I get to do what I want with it."

Dad's lips tighten. "All I'm asking, Dino, is that, as you explore your interests, you don't close yourself off to this one. Go see what else you might want to become, but always know that this door isn't closed to you."

"If this is about the name, if you're still holding out hope I'll eventually work here so that you can keep the name they way it is, I can tell you now, that's not going to happen."

Dad reaches into the inside pocket of his suit, pulls out a folded set of papers, and hands them to me.

"What—"

"I had these drawn up months ago. Not because you didn't want to work there, but because Delilah does."

I unfold the papers, and it's a lot of legal stuff I skim past, but in bold type I find the request to change the name to DeLuca Family Funeral Services.

"Does Dee know?"

"She will at the wedding," Dad says. "I wanted it to be a gift to her as she starts a new life."

I stare at the papers and then at my dad. "Then why have you been riding my ass about becoming a mortician when I haven't even graduated high school yet?"

"Language."

"Sorry."

Dad's shaking his head, and I know that look of frustration he's wearing. He gets it when he's tied up and doesn't know what to say. Usually, this is the part where Mom jumps in to help him, but he's on his own this time.

"I don't get you, Dino," Dad says. "I never have. I support you being gay, but I don't understand it. You play video games and do theater and work on stuff I don't comprehend. We've never had common interests. You've always been your mother's son." He stops and looks at me. "Not that I'm complaining. I'm glad you got the best of her, because even her worst is better than my best."

"You're rambling, Dad."

"DeLuca and Son's wasn't about the name for me. It was a dream. *My* dream. One thing we'd have in common. One area where I'd have something to teach you. Lord knows you're smarter than me in everything else."

"You taught me how to tie a bow tie," I say.

Dad chuckles. "Score one for the home team."

"Is that a sports reference?"

"Football, maybe?" he says.

I never knew my dad felt so left out. And it doesn't make me want to be a mortician, but hearing what he had to say does make me see him differently. "How about I teach *you* some things?" I say.

"What—"

I grab a controller off the floor, toss it to him, and turn on the TV. "How do you feel about piloting spaceships?"

DINO

DAD TURNS OUT TO BE A PRETTY DECENT PILOT, AND HE almost makes us late to the church when he picks a fight with a Thoraxian pirate squadron. We're in the middle of kicking their afts, and Grandma Sue finally grabs him by the ear and drags him out.

The service is sweet. Dee looks gorgeous walking down the aisle in her dress, but Theo can't stop crying, and it's so adorable that everyone's watching him and not Delilah, and I can see in her eyes that she's wondering if she can rewind us so that she can walk again and get the attention she deserves.

I stand with Delilah; Will stands with Theo. Will drops the rings. Grandma Jodi's sobbing so hard that Father O'Shea stops three times to let her get it out.

The "you may kiss the bride" moment comes, and Delilah dips Theo, which is going to make a great cover photo for their wedding album. Someone—I'm not saying who—decorated the back of the limo with rubber severed hands. The sound they make when being dragged down the street isn't nearly as satisfying as clinking cans.

And that's it. My sister is married.

DINO

"WHERE'S ROXY?" RAFI'S ARMS ENCIRCLE MY WAIST AND his forehead is pressed to mine as we dance to a slow number from Dee's playlist of faux-deep emo songs she dredged up from her past. We're both a little sweaty from being forced to dance to a horrid song called the "Macarena," and I don't even know what an electric slide is, but weddings seem to be a time when grown-ass adults act like they didn't have their hips replaced last winter.

"Uh . . ."

If I say I haven't been thinking about July since I left her at the beach, I'd be lying. But it's like thinking about climate change—I know it's important, I know it could affect the rest of my life, I know I should be searching for her or investigating the cause of her inability to remain dead, but I have no clue where to begin. Hell, I don't even know if she's still not-dead or if she's dead-dead again. So every time she barges into my thoughts, I push her to the side, figuring I can look for her after the wedding. The only concession I've made is to keep my phone on and with me in case she calls.

Rafi tilts his head so he can look me in the eyes. "She wasn't your cousin, was she?"

"If I say no, are you going to follow that up with a bunch of questions about who she was?"

"Probably."

"Then of course she was my cousin."

"Does this have anything to do with why your hands are covered in Band-Aids?"

"Couldn't say."

"Will you tell me the truth someday?" he asks.

"Maybe when the statute of limitations runs out."

"On what?"

I shrug. "Whatever."

Rafi grins and rolls his eyes, but I can sense that he's not quite certain whether I'm joking. It's best to let him assume whatever his imagination is cooking up. Rafi's sweet, kind, he looks good in clothes, and he assumes the best of everyone, so I doubt he'll ever come close to guessing the truth.

"July would have loved this," I say. I'm not sure what made me bring her up. I think, no matter what—whether we're friends or enemies, whether she's dead or not-dead—she's always going to be in my head, demanding I pay attention to her. It's kind of who she is.

Rafi squeezes me tighter. "Would she?"

"Definitely," I say. "Like, this was totally her thing. The chance to mingle and make a fool of herself for the amusement of a large, captive audience? She would have been on the dance floor for every song. Except during the cake cutting."

"July liked cake?"

"July *loved* cake."

"What kind was her favorite?"

"The kind with cake," I say. "Weren't you listening?" I laugh to myself thinking about it. "Every year, her mom had to make two cakes for her birthday. One for July and one for everyone else."

Rafi snorts. "You weren't kidding."

"She took it very seriously."

"What about pie?"

I shrug. "She'd eat it if she had to."

The song switches to a country song I've never heard that I assume Theo picked out, and I lead Rafi off the floor to an empty table. I remembered to wear an undershirt this time, so I strip off my jacket and hang it on the back of the chair.

"How come you never brought July around?" Rafi asks. "I always thought it was weird that she was your best friend but that we never met."

"We were fighting," I say.

Rafi leans into me. "Yeah, but before that."

"Worlds colliding."

"Sorry?"

There's a mostly full flute of champagne sitting on the table, begging me to drink it, so I do and hope that the person who started to drink it doesn't have the plague. "Weren't you the least bit scared to introduce me to your friends?"

Rafi shakes his head. "No."

"Like, you weren't worried they'd like me better or that they'd hate me or that I'd insult Kandis and you'd have to break up with me or date me in secret?"

"Were you worried about that with me?"

I sigh. "No. Because you're awesome. And July's awesome too. I had this perfect relationship with July. She knew me and I knew her, and we had routines and places and activities that belonged to us. Late-night dinners at Monty's and going to see weird plays and movies together. Then we met and I really, really liked you. You were different than July, and I enjoyed the time we spent together, but I didn't want to give up my little world with July either. I liked having my worlds separate."

"Oh," Rafi says. "I guess I get that."

"Do you?"

"Yeah. That's kind of how I feel about ballet and school. Dance is mine, I don't have to think about you when I'm dancing, and I can escape dance when I'm with you. One day, if we're still together, I'll bring you into that world, but I can understand you wanting to keep your life with July to yourself."

The crack in the sidewalk grows wider, and a dandelion shoot yawns toward the sun.

We sit on the sidelines for a while and then there's cake and speeches and more dancing. My mom cuts loose with Rafi, and I knew he could dance, but not like *that*. It's hot because it's him, and it's awkward to watch because it's with my mom, and I've never been so confused in my life. Even though the bride and groom usually open gifts on their own after the wedding, Dad announces that he's changing the name of the funeral home, and this time everyone is staring at Delilah, who can't stop crying.

I don't think my parents have given up trying to recruit me into the family business, but I get the feeling they'll be okay if I forge my own path.

I'm in the middle of being grilled by my mom's cousin—or second cousin; I can't keep them straight and Dee only invited them for the gifts—about the grossest body I've ever seen, when my phone buzzes. I excuse myself, grateful for the interruption. Rafi's on the dance floor holding an impromptu dance class with a horde of older women who are watching him like they've forgotten he's only seventeen. I wave as I take out my phone to check my messages.

JULY: Meet me outside.

I'm going to kill her. She can't be here. I make sure no one is watching, then I slip out of the ballroom. The country club is a maze, and I get lost and end up in the kitchen before finally finding the front entrance. Standing off to the side is July, in the ugliest dress I've ever seen, holding two blue raspberry Slurpees.

She holds one out to me and says, "Sorry I'm late."

JULY

"WHERE DID YOU GET THAT AWFUL DRESS?" AT LEAST
Dino waits to ask until we've found a quiet place on the side of
the building under some trees with a view of the golf course and
houses at the far edge of the green. He slurps his Slurpee while
mine sits beside him and melts, and all I can do is try to enjoy it
vicariously through him.

I give him a twirl in the dress, which is weird and flowery,
too tight at the chest and hips, and not quite long enough. "Hideous, yeah?"

"Yes," he says. "Where'd it come from?"

"Zora."

The color drains from Dino's face, and I figure I better explain
before he passes out or loses his mind or whatever, so I tell him
how I called Zora and stayed with her and borrowed the dress
from her so I could surprise him at the wedding and say good-bye.

"How could you do that?" he asks. "It was one thing telling her the truth about you being not-dead, but now you've dragged her into this nightmare, and she could be spilling your secret to her friends or selling you out to some shady online magazine for a few bucks."

"She's not," I say. "She won't."

"But how do you know?"

I try to act nonchalant. "We're friends now. I have a friend other than you."

That seemingly short circuits whatever brainpower Dino's got left. He sits holding his Slurpee with his mouth hanging open.

"You have to trust me, okay?"

"Trusting you isn't the problem. It's Zora I don't trust."

"Well, I'm not asking you to trust her," I say. "Just me."

Dino sucks on the straw and pulls up the last of his Slurpee and then starts on mine. It makes me strangely happy that it won't go to waste.

"How was the wedding?"

"You missed the cake."

"Why are you trying to hurt me?" I ask. "What did I ever do to you?" I'm only joking, but I quickly say, "Yeah, don't answer that."

Dino laughs. The color's returning to his cheeks, which is good because I need him to be okay so that we can get through what's coming.

"What do you think my wedding would've been like?" I ask.

Dino inhales slowly and then exhales with a soft laugh. "You would've been a monster, of course, but knowing is half the battle, so we would have been able to handle you."

"I'm not that demanding."

"You must not remember your confirmation party in eighth grade the way the rest of us remember it."

"We had fun!"

"Mandated fun at regular intervals, followed by periods of enforced July adoration."

I know Dino thinks he's being funny, but I'm not laughing anymore. "Why is it that when a guy knows what he wants and goes after it and is proud of who he is, people call him a winner or a leader, but when a girl does it she's a selfish bitch?"

"That's not what I was saying."

"Maybe not," I say, "but the implication is clear enough." I pause, giving Dino the opportunity to tell me I'm wrong, but he doesn't. "You know how I always pictured my wedding? I pictured it small. Me, you, Jo, the guy I'm marrying, if necessary. *Maybe* my parents, but only if they agreed not to fight. There'd be a small service held in the nearest Catholic church to wherever we were, my wedding dress would be a simple but elegant thrift store find. The rings would be whatever. And then there'd be cake."

"No reception?"

I shrug. "Doesn't matter, so long as there's cake."

"Makes sense."

"And do you know why that's my ideal wedding?"

Dino shakes his head. "I really don't."

"Because weddings are supposed to be about celebrating the unification of two lives into one with the people you care about most. And you, Jo, and my parents are who matter to me. Not the dress or the rings or the reception." I'm standing in front of him with my hands on my hips, more worked up about this than I mean to be. "Fine, yes, I'd also be wearing a tiara."

I sit on the bench beside Dino, leaving space between us. I didn't mean for us to get so far off track. I only asked the question expecting we could have a laugh before getting to the hard stuff.

"Jealousy," Dino says.

"What?"

"You're not a selfish bitch, July. We're just jealous that you know what you want and aren't afraid to fight for it."

"Even you?"

"Especially me," he says. "Look how hard it is for me to tell my parents what I don't want. Imagine what it's going to be like when I figure out what I actually do want?"

"You'll be fine."

"Maybe."

A yawn spreads through me. They haven't stopped since the night at the beach. It's this overwhelming force that starts in my toes and ripples through my cells until it reaches my mouth and demands to come out. The only sensation I've ever felt similar to it was when I had poison ivy and I couldn't stop scratching even when Momma would sit with me and rub Calamine lotion into the rash. She finally had to duct tape three layers of socks to my hands.

"Why'd you come here, July?" Dino asks. The question catches me by surprise, but luckily, I have an answer ready.

"To apologize."

"You don't—"

I hold up my hand to stop him. "I was shitty and mean because I wanted what Rafi had. You. Not like you're thinking. I'm not in love with you. But I do love you, and I saw you and him running off to have adventures that I wanted to be part of. It was easier to pretend he was some guy you'd get sick of eventually and that it would be the July and Dino show again."

Dino's lip is trembling. "I'm sorry too," he says. "I wanted you there but I also didn't want you there, but it wasn't because of you—"

"I know."

"I didn't understand how to fit someone new into our lives, and I resented you for my own stupidity."

"Stop." I take his hand and lace our fingers together. "I thought the way for me to die again and stay dead was for us to let go of each other. And when you made up with Rafi, I figured you'd done it. But I was wrong. This last year of fighting proved that nothing could ever make us let go of one another. We were both idiots, and we might have stayed angry at each other for a while, maybe a long while. We might have become nemeses living in our secret underwater bases plotting increasingly grue-some ways to destroy each other for years. But that would have only proven how much we still cared. Eventually, we would have sorted it out."

Dino looks me in the eyes, and I see the moment when his anger and all the pent-up frustration disappears. I see the moment he lets it go and becomes *my* Dino again. He pulls me to him and wraps his arms around me and hugs me.

"I could never hate you forever," he says.

I hold the hug as long as I can. And then I let go. "I couldn't die letting you think I hated you."

Another yawn tears through me, but this one's violent, and I sway a little. My eyes flutter, and I use the bench to steady myself.

"You okay?" Dino asks.

I nod.

"This is it, isn't it? The end."

"I wouldn't be me if I didn't make a dramatic exit."

"What now?" he asks. "What do we do?"

Now for the hard part. "*We* don't do anything."

"But—"

"I didn't come here for help, Dino. I came to say good-bye."

Dino scrambles to put together an argument. "You still need me. How are you going to get into your coffin? Do you have your phone in case it doesn't work again? You'll need me to get you—"

"Everything's taken care of."

"But I'm not," he says. "Who's going to take care of me when you're gone?"

I lean over and kiss his forehead. "Suck it up, DeLuca. You can take care of yourself now."

That's my cue. I start to rise, but Dino's head pops up and he goes, "Wait!" He runs off before I can stop him, leaving me sitting alone and confused. Maybe I was wrong and Dino can't take care of himself yet. He's lost his mind and who knows what he's going to return with, if he returns at all. The yawns are coming faster now, and my eyes feel heavy. I text Zora that I'll meet her at the car soon. If I don't, I'm afraid I'm going to become dead-dead right here at Delilah's wedding.

I'm standing when Dino comes sprinting back. He's breathing heavy and sweating and his face is red.

"Here," he says breathlessly. He shoves a bag into my hand. Inside is the coral dress I stole from myself when I snuck into my house.

"Why do you have this?"

"I kept it in the car just in case," he says. "No one should have to spend eternity in an ugly dress."

I rush him and hug him one last time. "I love you, Dino. You're gonna be amazing."

"I love you too." He squeezes me and I squeeze him, and then a yawn breaks us apart, and I stumble away. My head is filled with words, all the things I want to tell Dino but don't, because he's my best friend and he already knows.

"Hey, July!" he calls. I turn and he's standing there with his hands in his pockets, smiling just for me. "Break a leg."

DINO

RAFI COMES AROUND THE CORNER OF THE BUILDING and perks up when he sees me. He trots the rest of the distance to where I'm still sitting on the bench. I don't know how long it's been since July left.

"There you are," he says. "Everyone's been looking for you. Something about a speech by the best man?"

I forgot I was supposed to make a speech. I have no idea what I'd say. My mind's been on July. It still is.

It takes me a few moments to make words. "Sorry. I just needed to be alone."

Rafi stands over me. "Do you still need to be alone?"

I shake my head and hold out my hand and pull Rafi down beside me. He wraps his arm around my shoulders as I start to cry. "I miss her so much."

My tears are loud and ugly, and I bury my face in Rafi's chest. The jags come in waves, and I don't try to stop them. When the space between them grows wide enough, Rafi pulls me tighter and says, "You could tell me about her."

So I do.

DINO

THERE ARE FIVE DEAD BODIES IN THE FREEZER. PLUS THE one on the table in front of me. Mr. Arjun. Aged fifty-three. Died due to complications from a quadruple bypass surgery. I'm supposed to make him look like he's fresh off a ten-day Caribbean cruise.

Mom's blasting one of her favorite songs and doing a dance we refer to as the "goth stomp," which isn't a particularly creative name, while she puts the finishing touches on Mrs. Johnson, aged forty-nine, died from pancreatic cancer.

Dad leans over me and makes a chirp of approval. "Nice job on the skin tone, but his smile needs to look slightly less like he won the lottery and more like he's found the peace of death and is looking forward to the next—"

I snap off my gloves. "Yeah, good luck with that. I have a date."

"Where are you and Rafi going tonight?"

"He's taking me to see a ballet."

Dad grimaces. "And you're going willingly?"

"I made him sit through *Hairspray* last weekend, so I kind of owe him." I edge toward the door.

"Hey, Dino," Dad calls. "Thanks for helping out. We never could've gotten through this without you."

I shrug. "It's only until Dee's home from her honeymoon. I can handle it." I wave good-bye to Mom and take off so I can change and shower before Rafi picks me up.

Dad wasn't kidding about needing my help. The night of the wedding, Mom and Dad got flooded with calls. Every funeral home in the area's been dealing with the backlog of death. I found the woman from the hospital, the one missing part of her head, among the names of the dead waiting for burial, and I also learned that the man who'd been hit by the car had survived. The "miracle" had given him the time he'd needed to get help and live. I couldn't find any information regarding the man who'd tried to take his own life, but I assume, since I didn't see his name among the list of the dead, that he changed his mind. I hope so, anyway.

It only took a week for the "miracle" to cycle out of the news. No one knew how to explain it, so they called it a coincidence and moved on. The president tried to take credit for it, calling it "the greatest miracle in the history of miracles. There's never been a bigger miracle than this one," but everyone knows by now that he's full of shit.

I set my phone by the sink and hop into the shower to scrub

the smell of death off of me, and I think about July. Not because of the smell of death, although that is kind of a trigger, but because it doesn't take much to get me thinking about July. I went to her grave after the wedding, and it looked like it had the last time I'd been there. I assume Zora Hood helped dig up the coffin and get July into it. I saw her after the show when I stopped backstage to congratulate her and Benji on their amazing performances. She didn't mention July, but her hands were covered in Band-Aids.

I squirt conditioner into my hand and rub it through my hair, and then I hear a ding from my phone. I almost slip and fall and break my neck trying to get to it.

It's an e-mail from July.

I don't even bother rinsing my hair. I grab a towel and wrap it around my waist and sit in front of my computer. My hands are shaking as I lift the lid and click the e-mail.

Dear Dino,

If you're reading this, then it worked. Thank God. If it hadn't worked, you'd probably still be smelling me right now on account of I'd be sitting beside you annoying you, trying to come up with another plan.

But I guess since you're getting this e-mail, then I'm definitely dead. You should've expected it. This was your stupid idea after all.

Right now I'm sitting in Zora Hood's bedroom, and she's torturing me by eating those little bagel pizzas I love so damn much. They're almost as good as cake. Almost. I'm planning to show up at the wedding tomorrow night and make a dramatic scene and tell you good-bye and that I love you and that you're my best friend and all that other crap. I hope I manage to say most of it and that we don't get sidetracked like usual.

Who am I kidding? Of course we'll get sidetracked. We're Dino and July. It's what we do.

Anyway, I hope I got to say everything to you I wanted to say, because this e-mail isn't for you. I've made you executor of the Past. My past. The end of the e-mail will contain log-in information. I need you to go into the account and send the letters I wrote to my parents and to Jo. You can read them if you want—I can only haunt you or whatever—but, don't worry, I didn't mention about my time among the not-dead. It's just a bunch of stuff I should've said when I was alive.

Well, that's it, then.

I love you, Dino. And even though I'm gone, I'll always be watching over you. Yes, even when you're in the shower.

Love,
July

P.S. There's a little something attached to the e-mail for you. I finally finished *The Breakup Protection Program*. It may not be the ending you want, but it's an ending, and if you don't like it, you can write your own.

It's killing me to wait to read how July tied up everyone's stories, but the first thing I do is log in to the Past and send the e-mails July wrote to her family. They don't deserve to have to wait one second longer than necessary.

Then I scroll to the bottom and find the file.

I click it open, pull my computer into my lap, and read until the end.

ACKNOWLEDGMENTS

I write the stories, but creating a book takes a family of dedicated folks, and I'm lucky to work with the very best.

Katie Shea Boutillier, my agent and friend, who has been cheering for Dino and July from the first moment she met them. And the entire team at Donald Maass, who are each and everyone one amazing.

Liesa Abrams, my patient editor and confidant, who helped me take this story from "It's kind of about zombies, but not really, and there might be other stuff" and transform it into the story of two best friends trying to find a way to say good-bye.

Over the course of nine (nine!) books, the entire team at Simon & Schuster has been there to guide me and support me. Before I started, I didn't realize how many people there were working behind the scenes to lay out the pages and design the cover and pitch my books to librarians and teachers and bookstores. Now I know, and they are legion. I'm exceptionally lucky to have the support of people who love what they do and who do it so well. They are my champions and my heroes.

My brother, Ryan, who gave me a quiet place to stay when I needed it to finish this book, and who loaned me "Good Morning, Voldemort," from his imaginary *Hairspray*/Harry Potter mash-up musical. And to his patient husband, Syrus, who put up with me eating all their Otter Pops.

ACKNOWLEDGMENTS

My dearest and best friend, Rachel, for her always thoughtful notes on how to make Dino and July's story even better, and for just continuing to be in my life.

My family, for believing. And my mom, especially, for asking, "Are you going to end the world again in this one?"

To all the librarians, booksellers, and teachers who put my books into the hands of the readers who need them. What you do is special, and I can't ever thank you enough for doing it. If I had my way, you'd all be millionaires.

Finally, thank you to my readers. Thank you for letting Dino and July into your hearts. Thank you for being a part of their story, for being a part of all my stories. Just . . . thank you.

ABOUT THE AUTHOR

SHAUN DAVID HUTCHINSON is the author of numerous books for young adults, including *The Past and Other Things That Should Stay Buried*, *The Apocalypse of Elena Mendoza*, *At the Edge of the Universe*, and *We Are the Ants*. He also edited the anthologies *Violent Ends* and *Feral Youth* and wrote the memoir *Brave Face*, which chronicles his struggles with depression and coming out during his teenage years. He lives in Seattle, where he enjoys drinking coffee, yelling at the TV, and eating cake. Visit him at ShaunDavidHutchinson.com or on Twitter @shauniedarko.